47thRoman Legion
Stickmen

By I. Sylvano
Copyright © 2019 by Sylvano

ISBN: 9781794438064

For Aaja

This is a work of fiction.
This Roma is a different Roma.
The time is different, the sky is different and remnants of the old races still live.

More books by I Sylvano

**47th Roman Legion
War With Astibul trilogy**

Red Dust
Green River
Grey Cliffs

stand alone novels of the 47th Legion

Luka
Stickmen
Dogs of War
Dorian Falls

other books

Hold The Line   *war*
Bloody Blue Skies   *Military Fantasy*
The Red Handkerchief   *Police Mystery*
The Red Brassiere *Police Mystery*

Stickmen

Chapter 1

He was fourth in line and his mouth was completely dry because he was getting ready to lie about everything. He was actually a very good liar. He lied all the time. He had to. His father liked to punch him and what could he do to stop him? He was sixteen, tall and built like a piece of string.

The line moved up and now he was third away from the recruiting desk. He didn't think the 47th Roman Legion *Vigilanti*, would accept him. He couldn't prove he was a Roman citizen because he actually wasn't. His father had fought as an auxiliary a long time ago and claimed he now had citizenship but it was probably a lie. His father lied about everything. Like father, like son.

Second in line now. He was sort of chewing, trying to get some spit back in his mouth. He tried to convince himself that he could convince them. He was clever. People believed the things he said. Well, some people. A few. Elonia did.

He was starting to sweat now. Drips were running down his sides under his tunic, coming from his armpits. How was it possible that his mouth could be so dry while his armpits were dripping? He had to make this work. If he didn't, his father would kill him. Not punch him, or scold him, but kill him. Stab. Strangle. Choke. He'd found his father's stash- all the money the family had. Mother was dead. It was just his father and the three sons. He was the oldest.

The person in front of him was gone and they were looking expectantly at him. A broad shouldered centurion with a red crested helmet standing beside a clerk at the table.

"Step forward!" the centurion barked.

"Name?" the clerk asked. He wasn't writing on wax but real parchment.

"Titus Fufius," the tall thin pale blond young man said.

"Can you prove your citizenship?" the clerk asked.

Titus glanced at the centurion. The centurion was glaring

back at him.

"I can, but I can't. My father was supposed to come but he's very ill. He was an auxiliary and received citizenship. He can come tomorrow or maybe the next day or the day after that-"

The centurion smacked his vine cane down on the table. The clerk nearly fell off his chair.

"How old are you?" the centurion asked.

"Eighteen and two days. I just had my birthday," Titus lied. "Do you want me to fetch my father now? I can drag him here but it might kill him."

The centurion narrowed his eyes. "You don't look very fit."

"I'm very fit," Titus lied. "I'm known to be fast and don't let my skinny arms fool you, I'm very strong."

Both the centurion and the clerk looked doubtful. But the truth was that there was trouble brewing, and they needed to fill the ranks as best they could.

The centurion pointed his vine cane at another table off to the side. "Go there."

"Yes sir, thank you sir," Titus said and moved away as quickly as possible. He'd done it! He'd bluffed his way through!

It was not a clerk at the next table but a bored looking soldier of some kind. He didn't look like a Legionnaire because he wasn't wearing any armour. They had to take their armour off some time, didn't they?

"Name?" the bored soldier asked.

"Titus Fufius."

"Cognomen? Are you a citizen? What's your third name?"

"I don't really have one," Titus said. "I just turned eighteen and my family is poor and I usually stayed at home and worked on the farm."

The soldier wrote something down on the parchment. Then he turned it to face Titus. "Can you write? If not just make an X."

"I can write." Titus fumbled the pen and smudged ink on the scroll. He printed out Titus Fufius in careful letters. Then he noticed that the soldier had written his name above and given him a third name- Ramusculus, which meant 'twig'.

"Um, that's not the cognomen I'd want," Titus stammered.

"Too bad. It's yours now." He quickly rolled the scroll up and deposited it in a wooden box beside him. "Report here tomorrow morning at sunrise. Got it?"

"Yes, thank you, yes." Titus stepped away. He was in! His father wouldn't be able to lay a finger on him! He'd be protected by a whole squad of other Legionnaires. He'd learn to fight, with his fists and weapons and then his father would be afraid of him. He knew his father was a coward. Cowards back down when you stand up to them. He was going to learn how to do that.

Carefully, he stepped away from the crowd at the recruiting tables. He'd have to hide out for the rest of the day. It wouldn't be that hard – Dertona was a medium sized town. His father didn't even know he was here. He looked around. No one was paying any attention him. That was one advantage of being tall and really skinny. People ignored you. At this moment he couldn't think of another advantage, but that didn't matter. He had time and he was going to see Elonia.

Chapter 2

Titus was picturing Elonia as he walked. Remembering the huge smile on her face as he presented her with all the money he'd found in his father's stash. She was short and curvy- the exact opposite of him. She had long dark hair and dimples when she smiled. Her family hadn't approved of him so they'd always met in secret. Then her family had financial troubles- her father was a business man of some kind, and the recent unrest in Yallick had caused great problems. He'd invested in caravans, Elonia had said, and the crazy Yallick tribesmen had attacked the caravans and stolen everything. With the money from his father Titus had saved Elonia's family. They'd pay it back. He knew they would. He'd do anything for her. He was hopelessly in love.

Too in love to pay attention to what he was doing.

"Titus!" an angry voice called from behind him.

Titus was in such a romantic cloud he'd temporarily forgotten everything else. He turned, smiling, to see the furious red face of his father. Maxim Fufius' fist were balled and his face was red with anger. Titus began to back away quickly. His father grabbed him by the tunic and began shaking him. His mouth was moving but the man was too angry to form actual words. Instead it came out as a loud foamy growl.

Skinny young Titus tried to twist away but his father didn't let go and they both tumbled to the ground. They were both on their sides until his father pushed Titus flat and sat on him.

"No one steals from me!" he roared and drew his fist back to punch Titus in the face.

At the last moment the son wrenched his head to the side and the father's fist connected solidly with the paving stones underneath. The man's eye blew wide with the first rush of pain. Then he let go of Titus' tunic and began to scream. Using his legs, Titus tipped his father off, got up and ran. He knew the town well because he normally spent as much time as possible away from home.

He ran through the forum, past a large group of houses and ducked into a stable yard. The place rented and sold horses and wagons. Titus was found of horses and the owner was a nice man who'd let the boy brush the animals sometimes. The building was wood and there was a loft full of hay and straw. He ran to the ladder and scampered up. He crawled into a pile of straw near the edge of the loft so that he could keep an eye on who entered the yard, though he was fairly confident that his father wouldn't look here. His father might not look at all. Besides being a drunk he was lazy also.

Titus was dreaming about seeing Elonia, maybe actually kissing her, when voices below startled him. It was Jessop, the stable owner, with two men Titus didn't know. The men were arguing with Jessop over the price of a horse. Haggling was a normal thing but these men were arguing. Finally Jessop gave in and went to prepare the horse with saddle and reins. The two men thought they were alone.

"The Legion leaves tomorrow," the first man said. "You must go with it."

Titus couldn't see their faces, just the top of their heads. Both men had dark hair.

"I will," the other man said. "They've taken on a bunch of new recruits. No one will question me."

"Find out as much as you can about what they intend to do. You'll be contacted. Tell them everything. If it gets too dangerous, leave."

Titus was shocked by what he was hearing. Were they spies?

Jessop called to them and the two men walked towards the stable office. Titus wriggled right to the edge of the loft trying to see what the men looked like. He only was able to catch a quick glimpse of their backs. Their clothing was unremarkable but one of the men walked with a slight limp.

He was torn. He'd enlisted in the Legion- should he warn them? He was also shocked to hear that the Legion was leaving town. Titus hadn't known that. He knew that they'd go somewhere eventually but he thought that he'd be in camp for a while and he could visit Elonia and be protected from his father. Now he'd only have tonight to see her before they left. We won't be gone long, he tried to console himself. It didn't work and he still felt miserable.

When evening arrived he climbed down from the loft. He usually visited Elonia in the evenings. Her father was always out then, and Titus' own father had usually started on the wine then so it was good to be out of the house.

The town was still busy with people. There were a lot of taverns because the 47th Legion was stationed there. It looked like a lot of soldiers were in town. Some had families, or women, or were just having a drink. Titus moved carefully through all of them. He'd vowed to pay attention this time- this was important- he was going to see Elonia. He wondered if she'd cry when he told her that the Legion was leaving. He'd be back. He knew that she'd wait for him. She had such beautiful brown eyes.

He moved quickly once he was near her house. He knew the way so well he could have run it blindfolded. He arrived at her family's little home and did their secret knock, so she'd know it was him. Usually the door was opened right away. Tonight it wasn't. He knocked a second time, and a third. When the door was finally opened it was by Elonia's father. Titus had seen him before. He was a large dark haired man with intense eyes.

"I- I have the wrong house," Titus stammered.

But the man seized Titus by the tunic and pulled him in.

That's twice today I've been grabbed by the tunic. To his dismay Elonia was there too. She didn't look upset. Her father must have found out something; maybe she'd given him the money and he was going to thank Titus? Maybe Titus could ask for her hand?

"Don't come here anymore," her father said.

"Marco, let me do this," Elonia said. "Titus you're very sweet," she said. "Don't come here any more."

Titus' mouth was hanging open. No words came out.

"Marco's my husband," Elonia said. She stood beside him and held his hand. "If you come back or try to bother us, he'll kill you."

Titus felt like his face was imploding. Tears were blurring his vision. His legs were shaking.

Marco's face suddenly turned savage. "Get out!" he roared.

Titus just stood there so the big man pushed him out the door into the street.

It had all been a lie. He'd even seen her with other men before, but she'd always said that they were business associates of her father, or cousins. She was probably trying to get money from all of them.

He began to walk. He was crying, wailing. He hoped his father found him and beat him to mush.

Chapter 3

Jessop wasn't angry when Titus climbed down from the stable loft early the next morning. He just nodded his head good morning. Lots of people knew about Maxim Fufius Commotus, Titus' father. They didn't want to enrage the man but they didn't mind helping out his sons either.

Titus felt awful. He'd hardly slept. He'd waited until well after dark and then had gone back to Elonia's house. Crouched outside the door in the darkness. Heard her laughing, heard Marco laughing. They were drinking. They'd made a lot of money in one day. Somehow, Titus had found his way back to the stable. He almost went home- at least that's what he'd pretending to be thinking. The beating would have felt good. But he didn't go home, he hid in the straw again. See, he told himself, you lie even to yourself.

Young men were lining up outside of the 47th Legion's base. Titus stood back and watched them. He was taller than all of them, but they all were better built. Broad chests and shoulders, muscles-some looked like they'd been smith's apprentices. He tried not to draw any attention to himself as he went and stood with them. They were arranged in sloppy rows. Titus stood at the very back. He heard some of the others snickering at him. Looks like the Legion needed a new flag pole, someone said.

When the gates opened everyone stopped talking except some guy in the front row. You could tell by the sound of his voice that he was loud and stupid. Titus began to feel uneasy. *Are these really the people I'm going to be spending the next twenty-five years of my life with?*

"Finally!" front row stupid guy said. "It's not polite to keep us waiting."

The centurion that had come first out the gate marched straight to stupid loud guy. From where Titus was standing in the back row it looked like they were now nose to nose.

"I WILL TEACH YOU WHAT FUCKING POLITE IS," the centurion roared. He began beating stupid loud voice with his vine cane.

Stupid loud voice had the sense to collapse into a little ball, keeping his mouth shut. *Maybe he wasn't so stupid after all?*

When the centurion had finished beating the man, he turned to rest of the new recruits.

"We have very little time," he said very matter of factly. "If anyone else has any clever comments please say them now so that we can get that over with."

The ranks were completely silent. Loud mouth was still crumpled in a ball on the ground. A group of Legionnaires had come out of the gate and were standing at attention beside the centurion. The Legionnaires were all muscles and they moved like horses. In comparison the new recruits looked like chubby children. Titus looked like a very tall penis wearing clothes.

"Are we ready to get started?' the centurion asked.

Without a pause the Legionnaires shouted together. "Yes sir!"

"I was talking to them," the centurion smiled and pointed at the recruits. "Are you ready?"

A rather quiet low key "yes sir" answered.

The centurion was instantly in motion, running along the front rank. Some of the recruits actually backed up.

"DON'T BREAK RANKS! DON'T BREAK RANKS!" he shouted, striking left and right with his vine cane. "You will stay in line until you're told to get out of the line!" he howled. "You just have to say YES SIR like you mean it! Don't be a bunch of big babies! Now, are you ready?"

"YES SIR!" all the recruits, including Titus shouted.

The centurion smiled. "Now that's more like it!" It was disturbing the way he could change from being friendly to a roaring beast in less than a second.

"When your name is called, step forward and follow the soldier who called your name. Got it?" the centurion asked.

"YES SIR!" all the recruits answered.

The first Legionnaire stepped forward and read out several names from a wax tablet. The named men stepped forward and stood in front of the Legionnaire in a line. They then followed the soldier through the gates. The centurion watched it all, looking bored. Occasionally he made a critical face when a particular person would step forward- like the loud mouth he'd beaten. Titus was terrified of what the centurion was going to do when he stepped forward.

It never happened. The last Legionnaire called the last name and they marched through the gate leaving Titus and three others standing there.

The centurion smiled at them. "I think you can make a better line than that," he said.

Titus and the other three all moved at once, all trying to run to each other's spot to line up but it didn't work because they had all moved at the same time. They looked like chickens that were being chased.

"STOP!" the centurion shouted.

They all stopped so quickly that one older dark haired man actually fell over. He quickly got to his feet again.

The centurion pointed a meaty hand at Titus. He flinched.

"Form up on the stickman!"

Titus stayed where he was and the other three rushed over and stood beside him.

The centurion was still smiling. "That wasn't so hard, was it? Follow me."

He turned and went back into the camp. Titus followed and

the others trailed behind him like baby ducks through the big wooden gates of the 47th.

Chapter 4

The inside of the camp was nothing like the town outside. Dertona was a medium sized town with dusty streets and far too many bars and prostitutes- because of the Legion. There was a feeling of wildness about it, and it wasn't uncommon for there to be fistfights every night of the week. Titus had imagined that the whole world looked that way.

On the other side of the gates was a different world. All the streets were neatly laid out, the building well cared for, there was no litter on the ground, no dogs, no screaming children and no piles of excrement. The barracks and other buildings were neatly painted and well maintained. Legionnaires and officers walked around proudly or in groups all stepping together. It looked well organized and a little terrifying.

They saw no sign of the other recruits as they followed the centurion through the camp. Soldiers were constantly saluting the centurion and greeting him. He stopped so abruptly that Titus almost crashed into him.

"Stand at ease!" the centurion called out. When no one moved he frowned. "You don't know what that means yet, do you? Well, never mind; you will stand here until your section comes for you" He tapped the side of his helmet. "Remember, someone's always watching."

So they stood there at attention, at the side of the street. They looked ridiculous. They were having a hard time standing still and all were wearing civilian clothes. No one seemed to be taking any notice of them. They stood there until Titus thought he was going to fall down.

"Are we allowed to talk?" the young man beside Titus said. "No one's watching us."

"I suppose we can, I mean the centurion said someone is always watching. Until someone shouts at us I guess we're good," Titus babbled. "I'm Titus Fufius.

"Julius Mummius," the young man beside said. He looked even younger than Titus. His skin was smooth and there was no sign of whiskers. He wasn't as tall or thin as Titus, but he didn't look like Legionnaire material either.

The man beside Julius was built better. Average height, husky with dark hair and a neatly trimmed beard and moustache. "Tiberius Tadius Tenax," he said.

The last man was older and wore an eye patch. "I shouldn't have come," he said. "I'm too old for this. Lucius Cadminius Allec," he said by way of introduction. "You can call me Allec."

"Well now that we're here what are we supposed to do?" Tenax said.

"Wait!" Allec answered. "It's the name of the game in the Legion. Wait, wait, hurry, hurry, wait some more." He began to sing the words to himself.

Titus didn't recognize the tune, though admittedly he was no song wizard.

"Why did you join up?" Julius Mummius asked.

"To get away. You?"

"Same."

"Trouble follows you, you can't escape it," Allec said, ceasing his little song.

Tenax grunted disagreeably. "How about we try to act like grownups?" he said.

They continued to wait. After a time an officer came out of the building behind them. Instead of a bright red transverse crest on his helmet, he had a pair of raggedy yellow feathers on each side, like horns.

"Well, well, well," he said. "Look what the cat dragged in. Come with me."

The four recruits stood there uncertainly.

"I'm not going to shout quick march or something like that," yellow feathers said. "Just follow. And don't stamp your feet. Take nice steps. We don't hate our feet like Legionnaires do." The fellow went back into the building.

"You heard him," Tenax snapped. "I'm going in."

They all followed. Titus noticed that Tenax has a slight limp, like the man he'd seen in the stable. He had the same build and dark hair too.

The aura of order and organization vanished in the doorway. They were in an office, presumably, since yellow feathers was sitting at a cluttered dusk. There were a few clear feet in front the desk but every other space in the room was filled with piles, box, bags, creates. It wasn't well organized. It just looked like things had been heaped everywhere.

The soldier with the yellow feathers took his helmet off and clunked it carelessly on the desk.

"I'm Sedo," he said. "Who are you lot?"

Tenax frowned. "What is this?"

Sedo laughed and laughed. "It's the 47th Legion, mate. Where did you think you were?"

"It's just that- well- this isn't what I expected," Tenax said.

"It's exactly what I expected," Allec said with a smile.

Sedo smiled at him. "You look like someone's who played the game before."

Allec smiled. "I was a marker with the 11th Varaginian."

Sedo stood and clasped arms with the older man. "Pleased to meet you." He noticed the other recruits puzzled faces. "Didn't they tell you? It shouldn't be a surprise that you weren't selected to be Legionnaires," he said, rolling his eyes. "You're to be Libritors. The finest section in any Legion."

"What is that?" Julius Mummius asked.

Sedo laughed again. "You don't even know! It's the artillery, mate. You four are going to be playing with scorpions!"

Chapter 5

Scorpions. They were a class of smaller ballistae that used torsion arms to throw large arrows, like a giant crossbow. The recruits were out behind the building, which they'd discovered was artillery headquarters. Sedo was the optio in charge of the scorpions. There was also a ballista section, which shot bolts as tall as a man, and an onager sections for throwing rocks and really whatever you wanted to throw. In the past the scorpions had been operated by Legionnaires- one or two machines per century- but the newest legate wanted dedicated teams for the artillery. The legate wanted the heavy infantry in the front lines, not firing ballistae.

"Come on mates, let's get you kitted up," Sedo said after showing them the scorpions.

There was already a long line at the stores building.

"We'll wait until last," Sedo said, and sat on the ground against the wall.

The new recruits stood at the end of the line watching the optio. He waved them over to the wall.

"Do you want to stand? We could be here for hours," he said.

With a shrug Titus joined him and then the others did as well. Some of the recruits made angry faces at them. Sedo waved happily back.

"They think they're better than us," the optio explained. "So we let them think that. We're immunes- meaning we don't dig ditches or other stupid things. When it comes to fighting time they like us well enough. Even cheer for us sometimes. Then they go and get stabbed while we watch from behind. We've got the better job to my thinking."

It sounded good to Titus too.

"Any hoo, I'm officially your optio but you can call me Sedo. I know you're Allec, and you are?"

"Tiberius Tadius Tenax," the black bearded fellow said.

"We just use the last one in the Legion. 'Cause we're all mates. What about you?" Sedo pointed at the young man who sat beside Titus.

"Um, I'm Julius Mummius."

"No Cognomen?" Sedo asked.

Mummius shook his head.

"Well, how about Glaber? That's good for a start. Glaber- it suits you." Sedo laughed.

Glaber frowned, obviously not happy with the name. It meant *hairless.*

"When I signed on they called me Ramusculus," Titus said. It meant *twig.* It suited him and there were worse things he could have been called.

Sedo laughed. "See, we're all set then. Ramusculus, Glaber, Tenax and Allec."

The line leading into the stores building had moved quickly

while the Libritors had been chatting. Sedo jumped to his feet and led his four new recruits to the end of the line. Titus noted again that Tenax walked with a limp.

The inside of the stores building smelled like oil and fabric. The Legionnaire recruits in front of them were issued with metal segmented armor; overlapping plates that covered their shoulders and torsos. The Libritors were given lorica hamata- chain mail- instead.

"It's just like a tunic, see," Sedo said, as they watched Allec slip his on over the red tunic he'd been given. "You won't notice the weight and you can move around easier than in the plate armor."

Tenax had no problem being fitted but both Titus and Glaber were slight of build. The smallest mail hung loosely on them, and Titus' came only to his waist because he was so tall. They were issued heavy sandals, a scarf, under-padding, helmets and helmet liners, shields, gladii and other things. Sedo encouraged them to put it all on because it was easier than carrying it.

When Titus walked out of the stores building he felt like a different person. One who was carrying too much and probably looked ridiculous.

As Immunes they received better barracks than the Legionnaires. The four new recruits were put together in a room that would normally hold eight infantry men. They each claimed a bed and piled their new gear beside it.

"Now don't go getting too comfortable," Sedo advised. "I've heard we're marching out in a couple days. You four will share a tent. Your mates now, so look out for each other. Why don't you go have some lunch and then meet up with me after and we'll play with the scorpions a bit."

They all sat on their beds. Tenax looked angry.

"What's the matter?" Allec asked.

Tenax shook his head. "It just doesn't seem right. Sedo's so sloppy and relaxed."

"You could always ask to be transferred to an infantry century," Allec suggested.

"Not with my bad leg," Tenax said.

"You're quiet," Titus said to Glaber. "What do you think of all this?"

Glaber nodded. "It's good," he said. "It's perfect." Except he didn't look like he believed it.

Titus nodded too. It was okay. He had hoped to learn how to fight, to protect himself. He'd always been teased and bullied. But being behind all the fighting was a good thing too. Sometimes you have to focus on the good things Fortuna has given you and ignore everything else.

Chapter 6

Sedo had suggested that they collect their lunches and have a picnic. The recruits were shocked by this. Their idea of being in the Legion didn't really include picnics.

Sedo shook his head sadly. "Everything's a choice. We could stamp our feet and drill until your legs fall off, but what good would that do? You're not Legionnaires- you're Libritors." The optio's easy smile sagged into a frown and his eyes grew distant. "You'll see enough death soon enough. You should have every picnic you can while you still have the chance." He smiled again.

With their five wooden box lunches and waterskins they went to the rear of the artillery building. There were about fifty mules and half that number of wagons. And lots of artillery in pieces.

"You four are going to be section XII," Sedo explained. "Everything is labelled. Once we leave the camp everything labelled XII is your responsibility."

Allec had entered the mule corral. "I found XII!" he said happily, his smile showing his few teeth.

Tenax helped the older man get the mule out.

"Are you just going to stand there?!" Tenax thundered at the two younger men.

"We'll help," Glaber said nervously.

"We don't know what to do," Titus added.

Tenax looked exasperated. "Get the bloody wagon!"

The young recruits scrambled amongst the row of parked wagons and found the one labelled XII. They pulled it out and maneuvered over to where Allec was feeding the mule. Sedo watched everything, smiling the entire time. It took several tries but they managed to get the mule into the wagon traces. It was easy to see then that wagon was rigged for two mules. Allec opened the gate to go back into the corral but the mules were waiting for him this time and five ran out, knocking Allec down.

"Close the gate!" Tenax roared and did it himself.

They tried working in pairs cornering the runaway mules but the wily animals kept slipping passed them. Tenax got kicked in his bad leg, and Glaber took a bite on the arm that drew blood. At some point each of them ended up on the ground, which meant they were in mule shit. The first few times were annoying, and they tried to brush it off but after a bit they just gave up and focused on the job. Then they started working as a single team of four. They surrounded each rogue mule and forced it back to the corral, opened the gate just a tiny bit and pushed it inside. When all five mules were back in the corral the recruits were dirty and exhausted. And stinky.

"Did you look at the numbers branded on the mules?" Sedo asked.

They hadn't.

"You had the other XII out. You put him back in."

The young men groaned. Tenax swore. Allec looked like he was chewing something that didn't want to be chewed.

"I'll get the cursed thing," Tenax growled and slipped into the gate.

The mules had taken a dislike to the man and a few tried to kick him. He began to swear and shout. Allec entered carefully, making sure that no one escaped this time. Glaber and Titus waited at the gate. Allec found the mule with the XII brand and maneuvered it to the gate. Tenax pushed at it and Glaber and Titus opened the gate so just XII could get it out. They wrestled the mule over to the wagon where the other one was impatiently waiting, and hooked it up.

The recruits turned expectantly to Sedo.

He raised his eyebrows, surprised. "What are you looking at me for me?" he said.

"Can we go now?" Glaber asked.

Sedo laughed. "Oh, didn't I mention? This is a picnic and a training exercise. You're doing great so far." He laughed again. "But you forgot to load the wagon." He pointed at the pile of unassembled artillery pieces. "In future you should probably do the mules last. They don't idle well."

"You didn't tell us we were going to bring the scorpions," Tenax growled.

Sedo looked surprised. "You never asked. "That's just common sense, isn't it? If you don't know what you're doing, ask. This is the Legion. There's no shortage of people who'll tell you what to do."

"So we should load the scorpions into the wagon?" Glaber said, before Tenax could grumble some more.

Sedo smiled brightly and nodded.

They quickly found which area was reserved for the scorpions. They were wrapped in stiff waxed canvas to keep the moisture and rain out. There were four bundles marked XII and they loaded all of them into the wagons.

"What about ammunition?" Tenax asked.

Sedo nodded happily and pointed to a large shed. Glaber and Titus went in and grabbed ten bolts. They were wood with nasty metal tips, in total about three feet long with wooden fletching. They piled them into the wagon as well.

"Let's go," Tenax grouched.

The mules had been waiting for a long time and were in a cranky mood. One of them was willing to move and the other wasn't. Tenax looked like he was ready to hit the poor animal, so Allec stepped in. There was a kind gentleness about him, and he convinced the mules to work together. Soon the wagon was travelling along the neat cobbled streets of the base. They came to the main gate.

"We usually put a cover over the whole wagon," Sedo suggested.

Tenax snapped angrily. He'd had enough. "We're not walking back to get a bloody tarp!"

The Legionnaires at the door looked at the dark bearded man sharply.

"It's not good to shout at optios," Sedo said quietly. "It doesn't bother me so much but the infantry tends to take it rather seriously."

"Can we just go?" Tenax groaned.

Sedo shrugged and followed the wagon out the gate. It was

really more of a cart than a wagon- it was small, because that was easier to pull and to get up hills and between trees. The scorpions were heavy- it'd taken all four to lift each wrapped bundle into the wagon. There wasn't really any room for riders. The five of them walked beside and behind the wagon, Tenax limping slightly on his much kicked leg.

While they were still in the town everything was all right because the cobbles were fairly level. Once they hit the road things were more rutted and the scorpion bundles jumped and tumbled in the back of the wagon. Occasionally some of the bolts fell out.

The optio steered them a little way out of town into a field. There was a thick dirt wall at one end; it was the practice range.

"I'm getting hungry," Sedo said brightly. "How about that picnic now?"

Chapter 7

First thing they unhitched the mules and tethered them so they could graze. Allec really was very good with the two mules. Then they got out their own meals.

They ate in sullen silence. Lunch time was long past by now and they were all hungry.

Only Sedo seemed to be enjoying his food. "I think duck is better cold, don't you?" he asked.

No one replied.

"Well let's get to this then," Tenax said. He'd eaten hurriedly and was impatient.

Allec held up a hand. "In a few minutes," the older man said.

Everyone finished eating quickly. The unspoken thought that the sooner they finished this the sooner they could go back hung over everyone.

Together they unloaded the covered scorpion pieces and undid their wrappings. They were metal and wood and everything was coated with a fine layer of oil. There appeared to be two bases and two upper parts, where the torsion arms were.

"We need help," Tenax said to the optio.

Titus thought they could have figured it out but obviously Tenax was in a rush.

Sedo jumped up brightly and talked them through the assembly. The pieces had been cleverly made and quickly fitted together. The machines were chest height- or waist high on Titus. There were two winches at the back, which turned and pulled on the sinew ropes and two arms. The arms were made of layers of wood glued together. Once the winch had been wound back a pin was raised which held the rope in place. The ammunition- the wooden bolts, in this case, where placed in the channel. When ready, the pin was pulled down, the rope released and the tension in the arms shot the bolt forward. It all seemed simple enough, until they actually tried to do it.

"It can be fired by one person but it's faster with two," Sedo explained. "We've divided it into two jobs," the option continued. "The first job is called the marker. Allec, since you've done this before perhaps you'd show us?"

The older man nodded. He motioned Tenax over to help him. Each man worked one of the winches and turning together they ratcheted rope back. Allec then made adjustments to the angle of the scorpion- aiming it.

"It's the marker's job to aim," Sedo explained. "You see how Allec is looking though the center stanchions? That's where this bolt is going. Altering the angle changes the trajectory. With practice you should be able to shoot a man off a horse at 150 paces." The optio turned to Tenax. "The second job is called the stickman. After the scorpion has been winched, the stickman fetches the ammunition and then loads it into the channel."

Tenax grabbed a bolt and brought it over. He looked questioningly at the optio.

Sedo nodded. "Insert gently. If you bang things around there's a risk that the pin could let the rope go and if you're in the way it will probably break your arm, or worse, rip it right off."

Eyes wide, Tenax gingerly set the bolt into the channel and quickly stepped back. Allec released the pin and with a loud thwack the bolt was propelled out to shoot across the field into the dirt wall.

"That's a great first shot," Sedo said, smiling. He nodded his head at the two younger men.

"I can be marker," Glaber volunteered.

Titus didn't argue. They wound the scorpion and Titus grabbed a bolt and fit it into the channel. Glaber fiddled with the angle and pulled the pin. The bolt shot out, across the field and over the top of the dirt wall and disappeared.

"I hope there's nobody back there," Sedo said. He put his hand to his ear, in an exaggerated mime of listening. "No screams- must be okay. In battle, once the order to fire is given, you'll be expected to fire four times per minute."

They'd only brought ten bolts with them so each team fired four more times. Allec's shots all smacked into the dirt wall. Glaber fired one into the ground in front of the wall, another one over the wall and then the last two into the wall itself. Each shot took five minutes.

"Wasn't that fun?" Sedo said happily. "Now go retrieve the bolts. This is the Legion. We don't waste anything."

The four recruits walked through the field to the dirt embankment. Even though he smelled like mule shit, Titus was happy. For a little while he'd forgotten about Elonia and his own father and had just concentrated on ratcheting the winch back and loading the scorpion. It's possible, he thought, that he could be happy doing this. He looked over at the two older men. Limping Tenax and Allec, singing some song to himself. Titus was glad he'd ended up on a team with Glaber. He liked him, and Glaber seemed even tempered. Titus liked that they were both young and inexperienced.

Finding the bolt that had gone over the hill turned out to be much harder than one could have imagined. The land there was covered with scrubby forest and the bolts were nowhere in sight. Tenax and Allec quickly found the ones they'd shot in the dirt wall. Tenax carried the five bolts back to the scorpions and Allec came to help the young men. One bolt had penetrated a small tree trunk and had stopped half way through. It took all three of them to wiggle it out. Glaber finally found a groove in the ground that the other bolt had made. The arrow had ended by hitting a large stone. The metal head of the bolt was bent and the wooden shaft was smashed into a collection of splinters.

"That's one we don't have to bring back," Allec said with a cackle.

Titus smiled and looked over at Glaber. The young man was not smiling. He was staring at three tall figures who were watching them from the trees. Their faces were in shadow, and they all had clubs in their hands.

Chapter 8

"What's this now?" Allec said, regarding the three hostile looking figures.

Glaber had the bolt that they'd pulled from the tree. He gripped the end of it like a club, just like the three strangers were holding.

"What's your business here?" Allec called out.

The three men stepped forward. The one in front was Titus' father. Titus recognized the other two as his father's drinking friends.

His father looked very angry. "I'm here for what was stolen from me," he snarled. "By my no good lying thieving son." He swung his club threateningly through the air.

Allec and Glaber looked at Titus. Titus felt extremely warm, though at the moment he couldn't tell if it was fear or anger. Both probably.

"Where is it boy?" Maxim Fufius Commotus said. "Give it back and I won't break your legs."

"We're Roman soldiers," Allec said calmly. "Do you really think it's a good idea to threaten Legionnaires?"

"You three?" Titus' father laughed cruelly. "What are you, Legion bath boys? The Legion wouldn't take you." He emphasised the last with a spit. "I happen to know that Titus is both a weakling and a coward."

"Don't pull your sword!" Allec warned.

But it was too late. Titus had pulled out his gladius. Beside him, Glaber pulled his as well.

Titus' father and his thug friends looked serious now. This was no longer about beating a thieving son.

"I'll beat you until you tell me what you did with my money," Maxim snarled.

Titus gripped his sword tighter. "I gave it to a girl," he said. "Go ahead, come at me!"

Maxim advanced and so did his friends. Allec still hadn't pulled his sword. The thug in front of Glaber made a quick move and hit Glaber's wrist hard with the club. Glaber dropped the gladius into the leaves on the ground. Glaber began to back away.

"Go ahead, Titus, do something," his father goaded. "Do you have the guts? I didn't think so."

Maxim moved at his son. Titus held the sword out to block the club but Maxim's move had been a feint. He pulled out of it and struck Titus' hand. The blow was so hard he saw stars and his hand- momentarily out of his control- opened and dropped the gladius just as Glaber had done.

"You're not the first pretend soldiers we've given a beating to," Maxim said.

"But you'll be the last," a voice behind them said.

Everyone turned to see Tenax and Sedo behind the three thugs. Tenax had his gladius out and Sedo was holding a javelin.

"You've just made the worst mistake of your lives," Sedo said.

With a quick flick the optio threw the javelin. They all watched its quick flight as it sliced through the air and into the thug in front of Glaber, stabbing into his chest and taking him off his feet. Glaber gasped. With a few quick steps Allec was behind the other thug with his dagger and had it to the man's throat. The thug quickly dropped the club.

Tenax had advanced on Titus' father. His black beard and broad chest made him look frightening. Maxim snarled and rushed at Tenax.

"Don't kill him!" Titus shouted.

Maxim swung the club at Tenax's head. The Libritor raised his sword to block the blow but Maxim's move had only been a feint and he changed the angle of the club's attack. It turned out Maxim's parry had only been a feint as well for he quickly stepped forward and stabbed Titus's father in the chest just as Maxim was hitting him in the shoulder with the club. For a moment everything seemed frozen. Maxim was wide-eyed; he looked down at the sword in his chest. Then his eyes rolled back in his head and collapsed to the ground. Tenax wiped his sword on Maxim's tunic and resheathed his gladius. He began to rub his shoulder where the club had hit.

Sedo was frowning. "Two things," he said. "First, no one ever messes with anyone in this Legion. If someone bothers you, you'll have five thousand men at your back. If you see anyone bothering one of your mates, you'd better be at their back. Second," he continued, "You just made a whole lot of paperwork for me. I don't like paperwork. You will gather your gear and wait by the wagon for me."

Glaber picked his sword up and resheathed it.

"Allec, you and your prisoner will come with me," Sedo said. The three of them walked away.

Glaber was already on his way back to the wagon. Titus was in shock. He stood there staring at his father's crumpled body, and at Tenax, who was standing there with an angry look on his face.

"We were ordered back to the wagon," Tenax said, and limped away.

Titus looked down at his father. He wasn't sure how he felt. He'd been at odds with his father for as long as he could remember. Maxim had ruled their small holding with an iron fist. Titus and his brothers had suffered beatings and endless chores. But somehow, at this moment, he couldn't find any hate in himself. Maxim had been his father. He'd fed and clothed his three sons. Titus had stolen all of his hidden money. That's what had caused this. It seemed clear that the one most at fault was Titus himself.

He walked back over the hill. He could see Tenax and Glaber sitting beside the wagon. Somehow it was a comfort that they were waiting for him.

When he arrived Glaber spoke up. "Is she pretty?"

Titus looked up, confused.

"You said you gave all his money to a girl. Was she pretty?" Glaber said.

Titus shook his head. "No."

Chapter 9

After a while Allec returned. He had a basket of food and some water. He shared it with Tenax and Glaber. Titus didn't care if he ever ate again.

"Now what?" Glaber asked. "Do we go back?"

Allec shook his head. "We were ordered to wait by the wagon. So that's what we're going to do."

They eventually grew bored and decided to practice fire the scorpions again. Titus hadn't said anything. He ratcheted the winch and put the bolt in while Glaber did the aiming.

This time both crews fired all of their bolts into the hill. They collected them and cleaned the dirt off and prepared to fire again.

"Attention!" Sedo announced as he came up behind them.

The four recruits stood straight.

"You're to continue your training," the optio said. "Until further notice. Any questions?"

Glaber glanced at the sky. The sun was starting to drift towards the horizon. "Do you mean all night?"

"Sometimes that's what further notice means," Sedo said but he was less angry now. "Fire your bolts ten more times and then you can sleep."

"Out here?" Tenax asked.

"Yes," said Sedo. "Too bad you don't have a tarp. You could've used it as a tent." He turned and walked away.

The two crews continued firing. After the sun went down it became very hard to find the bolts in the dark. Allec showed Glaber how to shoot towards the same place every time. It made finding the bolts easier. When they'd finally finished ten times both moons were high in the sky. One of them was greenish, the other seemed a little purply.

"Green moon," Glaber said, pointing at it. "That means something bad will happen."

"Aye, but the other one's purple," Allec said. "Something good will happen, so it balances out."

They'd covered the scorpions with their covers.

"They're fussy," Allec had warned them. "Get 'em wet or too hot or too cold and they won't shoot worth two straws."

The four of them crawled under the wagon to sleep. The two mules were still grazing nearby.

"We'll take turns on watch," Allec said. "I'll go first."

Titus lay under the wagon and listened to Glaber snoring softly. He couldn't find sleep. When Allec touched his foot he stood up to take the second watch.

The night was bright under the tinted moons and stars. Titus saw a deer come out of the trees, look at them, and then dash back to the safety of the leaves. Then he heard an owl hooting. He got that odd sensation that someone was watching him. He looked around but could see no one. He looked at his comrades and saw the whites of Tenax's eyes.

The black bearded man crawled out from under the wagon and stretched stiffly. "Going for a dump," he said.

Titus watched his comrade limp into some nearby trees. Then there was silence. He had the awful feeling that Tenax was a spy and had gone to meet someone. When Tenax finally returned he didn't say anything to Titus, just crawled back under the wagon and closed his eyes.

Titus realized he didn't have the slightest idea when his time was up. Probably experienced soldiers could mark the passage of time by the movement of the moons. What if it was cloudy?

Eventually Glaber stood and came over.

"Allec kept elbowing me," Glaber explained. "he kept saying *watch, watch.* I thought he was going to do a trick or something." The young man placed a gentle hand on Titus' shoulder. "You couldn't have stopped it," Glaber said. "Your father was very angry. He's as much to blame for this as you."

Titus just nodded because he had nothing to say and went over to the wagon so he could pretend he was sleeping and not have to talk about this terrible thing that was his life.

Sedo came and got them in the morning. He brought them a breakfast basket. Titus had never been on so many picnics in his life.

"How'd you sleep, mates?" Sedo asked.

They all grumbled in reply.

Sedo smiled. "You won't forget the tarp next time, will you?"

Instead of going back to the artillery storage area Sedo stopped them at another building. It was some kind of meeting hall. Titus didn't know what it was. He hadn't paid attention at all. He'd just been following.

There was a table at the front of the room, with two chairs behind it. The rest of them sat on benches facing the table. Looking around, Titus noticed his father's thug friend sitting on the far left. At the back, much to his surprise, he saw his younger brothers. Their eyes met but Titus couldn't tell what they were thinking. They looked scared.

"Attention!" A Legionnaire at the door said loudly.

Everyone stood. A middle aged centurion strode into the room. It was clear from the way he walked that he was in charge. The metal of his armor and helmet shined and his red crest stood proudly. He went behind the table. Another man, a clerk, joined him there, with a stylus and wax tablets for taking notes.

"You may be seated," the centurion said. He took his time looking around the room. "For those of you who don't know, my name is Gaius Nellus Castus, senior centurion of the 47th Legion. You may be seated."

It was a hearing into what had happened.

Maxim's thug friend testified that Titus had stolen his father's money, and that his father had come to confront his son to get it back. Allec told how the three men had come at them with clubs. Optio Sedo, standing at attention and looking straight ahead, told how he'd tried to warn Maxim away. Tenax recounted how Titus' father had come at him with a club. Finally, First Spear Castus asked Titus to stand. He did as the other soldiers had- staring straight ahead at attention.

"Libritor, did you steal your father's money?

"Yes sir."

"Did Libritor Tenax kill him in self-defence?"

"Yes sir."

"Resume your seat."

Titus sat again, both relieved and worried at the same time. He knew from stories that Legion justice was harsh.

The clerk beside the First Spear had been quickly jotting notes through the entire proceedings. He stopped now as Castus looked out at the assembly of soldiers and civilians.

"There are two charges here," the centurion began. "First we find the Libritors of XII section defended themselves when attacked. Let all citizens beware of antagonizing the Legion. Second, this seems a family dispute. The father is now dead. The son had enlisted in the 47th. The dispute is finished. There are no charges. We're finished."

The soldier at the entrance way called everyone to attention and First Spear Castus made his exit. After he was gone everyone relaxed and began to leave.

"I will see you all back at artillery," Sedo said and left.

Glaber gave Titus a congratulatory smack on the back. Then he left with Tenax and Allec. Maxim's thug friend had also left. He'd been one of the first to leave. Titus stood there, waiting. When he turned around only his younger brothers were left. They met in the middle of the room, in the aisle between the benches. They held onto each other. Appius was fourteen, Tullus was only nine.

"I've joined the Legion," Titus said.

"We noticed." Appius replied. He was always a bit of a smart Alek. Many of their father's rages had been focused on Appius.

"Stay on the farm," Titus said. "You did all the work anyway."

"*We* did the work," Tullus said.

"I'll send you money. Be good. Don't be like me."

Tullus began to cry.

Titus hugged him close. "Don't worry. I have to go away with the Legion, but I'll be back soon."

His brothers looked at him. They didn't believe him.

Chapter 10

The next morning the 47th Legion *Vigilanti* marched.

Titus, the rest of XII section, and all of the other Libritor sections were still packing their wagons while the Legionnaires headed out of the camp. The noise was incredible. Marching feet in step, armor jangling, the cries of the centurions- all filled the air, which seemed to be crackling with energy. Titus was able to see the rest of the Libritors; he wasn't sure what he'd expected but they were much like section XII- older, younger, skinny, limpy. Sedo arrived on a horse in his full armour and feathered helmet. Apparently he was in charge of all twelve sections and twenty-four scorpions.

Glaber, Titus, Tenax and Allec waited patiently by their wagon as the other sections pulled out of the artillery yard onto the cobbled street of the camp. Finally it was their turn. Allec convinced the mules to start moving with some gentle words and away they went. All of the section XII members except Titus had brought a bag or pack along, stowed in the wagon. Titus didn't have anything to bring except what he'd been issued.

The long column left the camp, wound through the town and then out along the good Roman road. Section XII had not forgotten to bring a tarp. They'd been issued a tent as well. Behind them was the baggage train; hundreds of mules and wagons filled with food, tents and equipment. One of the Legion cohorts was the rear guard.

The travelling was pleasant. There was no dust from the those in front because they were on the road. Most of the animals had emptied their bowels at the beginning so the road was almost shit free. The air smelled of oil, sweat and mules.

It was nice to be away, Titus thought. He'd been trapped for so long at home with his father. The girl Elonia had been a distraction. For a while he'd thought she'd been an answer and he'd dreamt of running away with her. He shook his head, as if doing so would clear his past from his brain. For a moment in his mind he saw his father's dead body. And his two younger brothers' faces. He tried to shake away those images too. He was in the Legion now, and there was no escape without penalty. They were walking away from Dertona and somehow Titus hoped that this was a new beginning for him.

The rest of section XII walked in silence as well, all lost in their own thoughts. Glaber was looking around at the rolling grassy country side, as if he'd never been anywhere before. Allec was singing some song to himself. Tenax looked angry, limping along. Maybe his leg was causing him pain.

It was obvious Tenax had fought with a sword and even killed before. *Why had he joined up?* Titus accepted that there could be a hundred different reasons. Also a lot of men had black hair. Many had limps. It didn't mean that Tenax was the spy. At this moment it didn't seem that important. Tenax was the man who'd killed his father. *Yes, it had been self defense.* If Tenax and Sedo hadn't arrived Maxim would have beaten, possibly killed Titus. But sometimes things just don't add up no matter how many times you try to force them to.

They walked for four hours. The pace wasn't bad. Allec said the Legion was taking it easy at the start and they wanted to stay with the Libritors and the baggage, so really the mules were setting the pace.

They halted for lunch. Allec left the mules hitched but drove them to the side of the road so they could graze. The countryside was beautiful. Dertona was out of sight now, but there were small farms and fields all along the road. Beyond that there were immense stretches of grass. Sometimes there were flocks of sheep, or cows, and once in the distance they'd seen an immense herd of deer.

As they sat eating, a short balding man from one of the other Libritor sections came over and sat with them. He smiled a gaped tooth smile.

"I'm Mergo, from VIII section."

Allec shook hands with him. "Welcome to the elegant dining room of XII section."

"Do you know where we're going?" Glaber asked the newcomer.

He shrugged. "Yallick. One of the border tribes is making a fuss, I guess, so we're going to try and calm things down."

"Swords are good for that," Allec quipped.

"You're all new?"

They nodded.

"I've been in for more than a year but haven't seen any action yet." He rubbed his hands together. "I'm tired of shooting at piles of dirt. I want real targets."

"The problem with real targets is they won't keep still," Allec laughed. "Dirt piles are easier, and they don't shoot back."

"I'm pretty sure the troublemakers don't have artillery," Mergo said.

"They've got arrows," Allec nodded.

Mergo looked directly at Tenax, who'd said nothing. "You're a quiet one."

"So?"

"No issue," Mergo said, backing off, "I just wanted to be friendly. After all, we're all in this together."

Tenax didn't say anything.

Horns sounded and it was time to get moving again. Titus

could see things moving up ahead but it took a while before they had opportunity to move themselves.

At some point over the next seven hours the travelling lost its amusing qualities. Titus' lower legs grew sore, and his feet blistered in his new boots. There was little to see except grass and a few copses of trees. There were still a few farms along the road but they were far between. They'd eaten a cold supper on the march. Then there were no more farms; nothing but brown grass and more brown grass, waving like the sea in the wind.

Titus felt pressure in his abdomen and knew he had to poop. He'd watched other soldiers crouched by the side of the road. He didn't want to do that but eventually he could wait no longer. He left the column and almost stepped in someone else's poop in the grass. He'd crouched and waited. Every single person who passed looked at him. He was embarrassed, in bare ass. His poop wouldn't come out. He ran to catch up with section XII.

Everyone was relieved when they finally halted for the night. They unhooked the mules and fed them and then left them tethered near the wagon to graze. Sedo explained that there'd be no marching camp tonight because they were still far from the troubled area. Section XII set up their tent and all four of them collapsed into it, exhausted. Libritors didn't have to stand watches because they were Immunes. Staying up half the night staring into the darkness was an infantry job.

As tired as he was, Titus lay awake. The tent flaps were closed so it was dark inside. Tenax was snoring and Allec breathed in and out with a small whistling sound.

"You awake?" Glaber said very softly.

"Yes."

"I have to take a dump," Glaber continued. "Do you want to come?"

"Yes."

They quietly exited the tent, careful not to disturb their section mates. Outside the sky was dull dark grey with clouds and no moons or stars.

"I don't usually invite people to poop with me," Glaber said. "but I saw what happened today. I wasn't watching you- you dropped out and you were holding your stomach. When you came back you were still holding your stomach."

"Yea," Titus admitted, "it's hard when everyone is staring at you."

"You didn't see me holding my stomach?"

Titus laughed. "I was too busy thinking about my own problems."

The two Libritors went to the edge of the camp. The Legionnaires on watch laughed when they were told what the trip was for but it was a friendly laugh.

Under grey clouds on a dark night with his friend Glaber nearby, Titus had his first Legion field poop.

Chapter 11

Titus dreamt of his father that night. Maxim was coming home, his arms loaded with groceries. He came in the door and looked sadly at Titus.

"This is all I could get," Maxim said, "because the money is gone."

Titus knew that he himself had stolen the money and given in to Elonia. He tried to convince his father that he still had a lot of food – his arms were full. Maxim wouldn't listen. Instead he dropped everything onto the floor and grabbed Titus around the neck.

When Titus opened his eyes he was in the tent he shared with XII section and his own arm was up, his hand resting on his face. An immense sadness filled him. He pictured his brothers on the small farm. He would send them money, all that he made. Pay was issued quarterly so there was still months to wait, but he'd send it.

He thought of Elonia too. Not the good times; in fact, he'd begun to wonder if there actually had been any good times. Most of it had been in his head. Hope for the future, the idea that she loved him- she'd just lead him on. She'd said little, mostly smiled coyly, blinked her beautiful eyes at him. There was no pleasure in those remembrances now. Overtop all of it was her voice saying *don't come back here anymore. Marco's my husband.*

In a matter of days everything in his life had been destroyed.

He himself had wrecked it. By being stupid. Lastly he pictured his father's crumpled body lying in the leaves, and Tenax wiping the blood from his sword on his father's tunic. Yes, the Legion would stand up for him. But he wasn't worth it. It would be better if he were dead. Maybe he'd die in the coming battle? It was something to hope for- an end to the pain that was burning his insides.

The horns sounded and Titus had no idea what they meant. They didn't sound desperate or excited, so it was probably just wake up, or whatever the Legion called it. He stepped out of the tent. It was still dark. The sky to the east had a hint of orange in it.

All around soldiers were grumbling and stumbling out of their tents.

"Cold breakfast!" someone shouted.

The horns sounded again, more insistent this time. The rest of section XII came out of the tent, stretching, groaning, rubbing a sore limpy leg.

"Let's get the tent down," Allec said.

He guided them through it. It was nice that he knew what he was doing. They shared some hard bread, cheese and water and went off to find the mules.

Titus was amazed at how quickly the small sea of tents vanished and became a wave of waiting soldiers. The mules were cranky. After a whole day of travelling they didn't want to be hooked to the wagon again. Allec sweet talked them, and when that faltered he began shoving them. Glaber helped.

Everything started moving. The sun was up over the horizon now. After travelling about half an hour, the column began to leave the road. A halt was called while the Libritors and their wagons were still on the pavement. In front of them the Legion reorganized, changing from a long column to a wider one. They started moving again.

Titus liked the moving, the walking, even though his legs were sore. It made him feel like he was accomplishing something. Moving away from recent events. The only problem was that he couldn't imagine a future.

The brown grass was tall, knee high ins pots. Titus had thought it was going to be fun moving through the long grass, more interesting that the stone road. He was wrong. Perhaps those at the front of the column enjoyed some fresh pleasure from moving through the tall swishing grass. Those behind trampled the grass flat, stirred up dust where the ground was dry and mud where it was wet and by the time the wagons got to it, things were a mess. There was dirt in the air, in Titus' mouth and all over his body. The ground had become rough and rutted and they had to stay with the wagon, frequently pushing and pulling through holes and furrows. Titus glanced behind and saw that the Legion was leaving a huge muddy gash across the land.

A halt was called at lunch and everyone sat by the wagon and rested and ate their walking ration. Allec made sure the mules had lots of water. Tenax looked exhausted. He was rubbing his bad leg. Glaber looked like he wasn't home- his eyes seemed empty and he was staring straight ahead, at nothing. I wonder what he's running from, Titus wondered. The young man had only shown kindness and Titus considered him a friend. *But why had he joined the Legion? Were they all running from something?*

Horns sounded and they started moving again. Everyone was tired. No one wanted to open their mouths to talk because the air was so full of dirt. Sedo galloped by on horseback but he didn't even look at them. It was sunny and the light grew hazy from the dust. Titus began to sweat, especially when he was pushing the wagon out of rut. He was thirsty but he'd been warned not to drink too much of his water. There were limited chances to refill it.

Section XII was relieved when they halted. The Legionnaires began building a marching camp, digging out ditches and chunks of sod to form walls. Sedo arrived and ordered the Libritors to form up with shields and pila.

"Although you are immunes and don't assist in the constructions of the camp, you are not immune from drill," Sedo announced loudly. "I recommend you pay attention and try your best, for one day your life may depend on it."

Titus was too tired to try his best. They practiced shield walls, stepping and stabbing, throwing pila and holding their shield over their heads to protect them from arrows. The result was that Titus' arms now hurt as much as his legs.

The Legionnaires finished the camp in under two hours. The Libritors and their wagons trundled in the main gate to their assigned area. It was the same spot that the artillery headquarters was in back at the Dertona base. Every camp was set up the same, so you always knew where you were.

Mules and wagons were stowed and all of the Scorpion sections sat together to eat and listen to Sedo lecture.

"This is Niallus," Sedo introduced.

Niallus was a tall thin Libritor, similar in build to Titus but with dark hair. He was holding a long pole with a red and yellow striped pennant at the top.

"When Niallus holds the signum straight up, as he's doing now, that means stand by. Be ready, prepared to fire. Your scorpion should be loaded and aimed. When you see the pennant dipping and twirling, that's the order to fire."

XII section ate their bread and cheese and shared a skin of wine as Niallus waved the pennant. It all made sense. That way the entire group of scorpion sections could work together and receive orders from a distance.

"Once the pennant has dipped and twirled it may disappear from sight," Sedo continued.

Niallus lowered the pennant to the ground.

"If you can't see the pennant you are to continue firing. When it goes up again you stop and standby. When it leans in one direction that means start moving your equipment that way. The stickmen should keep an eye on the pennant. The marker is always aiming. Any questions?"

"What does retreat look like?" a libritor asked.

Sedo shook his head. "We don't retreat. If you see the pennant going straight up and down, that means pack up your scorpion and load your wagon. The pennant is your commander. You will follow its orders as if it were a centurion."

"What if we don't follow orders?" the same libritor asked.

"There's always room for a head on top of the pennant." Sedo said with a smile.

Chapter 12

They left the marching camp- the walls and ditch- intact when they departed the next morning. The gates and towers were made to disassemble and they brought them along for the next camp. The horns had sounded before sun up and section XII, along with everyone else, had been getting ready since then.

Rumour had it that the weather would hold. Summer here was stable- sunny, warm, and dry. They were approaching the big grasslands now- miles and miles of rolling grasses and occasionally small shrubs. There was not so much mud now, and more dust. The mule wagons didn't get stuck as often and that was a blessing. The soldiers all had their scarves over their mouths and noses to try and block the haze they'd stirred up in the air.

The Libritors were mostly quiet as they travelled. Titus wondered how many of them were new troops that were, like him, struggling to keep up. They could hear the Legionnaires in front of them singing, even with all the dust. Titus thought it might have been nice to have been at the front of the column. From there a person could see the countryside. The Libritors were only able to see the rest of the Legion marching through the haze.

They were allowed a halt for lunch and to feed and water the mules.

Mergo, the short balding Libritor from VIII section came over to eat with section XII.

"He's going to drive us hard," Mergo said, wrestling with a piece of stringing dried meat.

"Who is?" Glaber asked.

"The Legate. Marcus Lavinius Horatio. He's a hard-nosed bastard," Mergo said.

"It's difficult to be friendly in a war," Tenax observed.

"Better to be hard-nosed than dead," Allec added.

Mergo shook his head dismissively. "You haven't heard the things I've heard," he said. "He commanded the 32nd Legion in the Cardean War. They were almost entirely wiped out."

"I'm not interested in talk like that," Tenax growled. "So the 32nd was heavy in the fighting, what of it? That's what they were there for."

"I'm just saying," Mergo was starting to get defensive, "that we can expect a lot of hard marches."

Tenax was starting to get angry. "It's the fucking army! What did you think it was going to be?" He'd stood and given Mergo a shove. "Let us eat our lunch in peace!"

Mergo grumbled as he stalked off.

"I was in the Cardean War," Allec said.

Tenax stared at him. "And?"

"It was rough. But as you said, that's what war is."

Titus and Glaber looked at each other. It hadn't really sunk in for them that they were at war. They were going to be attacked at some point, and were going to be firing the scorpions, killing others. So far it had all seemed a big adventure with too much walking and boring food.

The horns sounded and they started out again. Titus had no idea where they were, or where they were going. His world had shrunk to the two mules, the wagon, and the unassembled scorpions wrapped carefully to keep them dry and clean.

The land became more rolling, and it seemed they were always either walking up a small hill, or going down one. Uphill was actually preferable because it was easier to control the mules and the wagon. When they went downhill the wagon wanted to roll faster, the mules felt the pressure and wanted to trot and if they weren't careful they'd smash into others or tip over.

The afternoon was hot. Again Titus had to consciously not consume his day's allotment of water all in one long drink.

They marched until evening and then halted. The Legionnaires began building a marching camp again, and the Libritors were drilled. Titus found his arms were quite sore from the day before. He saw Glaber grimacing and knew he felt the same. Tenax was always frowning so who knew what was going through his head. They practiced their shield wall, threw pila and went over step and stab a dozen times. They moved in formations to the left, to the right, and stepped through a walking retreat. Then they had to sort the pila and send any that had been bent or damaged to the smiths for repair. The javelins had soft metal heads so that when they were thrown the metal often bent on impact, making them useless to the enemy.

While they ate Sedo went over the pennant signals again, and did a demonstration about the aiming adjustments to consider when firing from hills or towards hills.

It was dark by the time they had free time and most soldiers were going to their tents to sleep.

"Do you want to go for a walk?" Glaber asked.

"Sure," Titus said. He was tired but he was also bored.

The night was cooler than the day but it was still sufficiently warm. They two Libritors went over to the turf wall and exchanged pleasantries with the Legionnaires on watch. The partial moons were bright above, floating in a sea of stars. There were few fires in camp and no torches, so their eyes found it easy to look out over the wall at the grassland. The camp had been made on a small hill and the surrounding bumps were not large enough to block the view.

"There's people out there!" Glaber said, pointing.

"Just some of ours," a Legionnaire answered. "We're still on *easy* status," he explained. "We're not expecting trouble yet," he said with a smile.

"Want to go out?" Glaber asked.

The two young men went to the gate and were allowed to pass. It was entirely different than being in the camp. The camp was like a city, full of sound and smell and other soldiers no matter where you turned. Fifty paces from the gate it was a different world. They lay down in the grass and looked up at the stars while the crickets chorused around them. The sky seemed deep, like an ocean without end. Laying in the grass staring upwards Titus felt very small and unimportant. *Were there gods in the stars looking down at him?*

Titus heard an owl hoot nearby and it distracted him. Did owls live in the grasslands? He didn't know much about them. He'd always thought of them as tree dwellers.

Glaber wanted to go back then so the pair headed quietly through the darkness to towards the gate.

"Did you see him?" Glaber asked.

"Who?" Titus said.

"Tenax. He was out there too. That's why I wanted to come back. I don't like him."

Titus nodded. "Neither do I."

Chapter 13

The next day was almost exactly the same. Up before dawn, a quick bite, packing up the tent and getting the wagon ready. Then leaving the camp behind and travelling through the trampled grass and dust up and down the gently rolling hills.

Titus still felt tired but it was like there were two parts to him now- the tired part, and another part which was able to think and talk while the tired part kept walking and doing what it was told to do.

Allec tried to teach them a Legion marching song until Tenax got crabby and made him shut up.

The day passed as the one before it had and soon the Legionnaires were building a camp in the evening as the Libritors drilled. Titus had wanted to believe that he was getting better with his sword and shield but he couldn't deny that his arms were even more sore and that he was struggling to keep the shield up for any length of time. When they threw pila, his pilum went the shortest distance. His face reddened with shame even though no one seemed to notice. Everyone was lost in their own tortured little mental worlds.

Sedo lectured them on the pennant again, and then made them unpack their scorpions and assemble them, ready to fire. Then they packed them up again.

When they were finished for the day and released to sleep as they pleased Glaber and Titus wandered over to the wall for a look. The camp had been built on a hill again and you could see for quite a long distance in every direction.

"Want to walk outside the walls?" Titus suggested

Glaber nodded and they went to the gate.

Tonight there was an argument happening. An angry Legionnaire was barking at another soldier.

"Legate's orders!" the Legionnaire snapped. "Gates closed, no one out without a written order."

"It's stupid!" the large dark-haired man growled.

Titus was surprised to see that it was Tenax.

"We're miles from the enemy. I just want to have some peace and quiet," Tenax continued.

"Go talk to your centurion," the Legionnaire said, and then turned really nasty, "and get the fuck out of my face!

Tenax stalked off angrily.

"Stupid Libritors," the Legionnaire cursed.

Then he turned and notice Titus and Glaber watching. The two friends quickly left. They went over to a different wall, far from that gate. There was a light wind and it made a faint rustling sound as it toyed with the grasses. Titus heard an owl hooting. A firm hand clamped onto Titus' shoulder. It was one of the Legionnaires on guard duty. He pointed toward a distant hill.

"Look!" the man said.

At first Titus didn't see anything but some bushes but then he realized that they weren't bushes. They were men on horses, about a dozen of them, watching the camp.

"Who are they?" Titus asked.

"Those are the enemy," the Legionnaire said.

Glaber and Titus went back to the tent. Allec was curled in a ball, snoring. Tenax wasn't there.

"Are you scared?" Titus asked Glaber. Titus wasn't sure if he himself was, but there was an uncomfortable feeling in the pit of his stomach.

"I don't know," Glaber said. "It was shocking to see the enemy, and to know that they're watching us. But I feel perfectly safe here surrounded by the Legion."

Titus nodded. *But what was that feeling in his stomach?*

They turned in for the night then. Tenax still wasn't there. Soon Titus could hear Glaber's soft regular breathing in between Allec's snoring.

It was the thought of the owl hoot that was keeping him awake. It was the same kind of hoot he'd heard before, and each time Tenax had been around, trying to go out into the night. He remembered hiding in the loft of the stable, listening to the two dark-haired men make their plans. One of them had a limp, like Tenax. He was worried. He was afraid that Tenax was a spy and would betray them all. That was the feeling in his stomach.

He had to tell someone. Not Glaber or Allec, they wouldn't know what to do. He decided to try to find Optio Sedo. That was the right thing. In the army you talked to the officer in charge of your unit, and then they decided want to do next.

Although most of the camp was asleep there were still many men awake. There was a raucous dice game happening between a pair of Libritor wagons. Titus looked for Tenax there but didn't see him.

Sedo shared a tent with Niallus, the Libritor signifier. Titus was nervous about talking to the optio- what if he was wrong? He decided that he'd check the tent and if Sedo was sleeping Titus would think about it some more and then make a decision the next day.

The flap to the tent was open. Sedo was not sleeping and neither was Niallus. It was a standard sized tent but because there were only two of them there was more room. They were sitting on ground with a lantern and were looking at wax tablets and scrolls. There was a third person in there too and Sedo was lecturing; they were discussing the maximum range of the scorpions. Sedo noticed Titus looking in the doorway and smiled.

"Ramusculus, isn't it?" the optio said. "Step in."

Titus ducked into the tent. They all looked at him expectantly; Sedo, Niallus, and Tenax; their faces lit by the flow of the lantern. Titus felt the knot in his stomach expand into something bigger.

"Did you have a question?" Sedo asked.

Titus couldn't think of anything to say. He shook his head.

"I just wanted to say goodnight." He stepped out of the tent.

Chapter 14

They know, Titus thought, staring up at the tent ceiling. Glaber and Allec were still sleeping. Tenax had returned and gone right to sleep. He was now snoring with Allec. *Do all older men snore?* Titus rolled onto his side. *I'm so stupid. Was Sedo part of the spy group?* Titus didn't think so, but then again he didn't really know. He was scared. He was shivering and it wasn't even that cold. Originally travelling with the 47th had felt like an escape, but now he felt trapped. They weren't allowed to leave the camp, the enemy was watching them and there was a traitor in his own section. Well, possibly a traitor. What if he was completely wrong about everything? For a moment Elonia's face flashed through his mind, only to be replaced with the image of his father lying dead on the ground. He crawled out of the tent and stood up, sucking in deep gulps of the night air. Stars and the two moons twinkled were overhead. Tents all around, and the reassuring sounds of others calmly snoring. For a moment he wondered why he'd ever joined up but then he remembered why. It didn't help.

He'd thought that he'd spend the night outside of the tent. He didn't trust Tenax- the man could be fake snoring- Tenax could crawl beside Titus and strangle him in the dark tent. He hadn't considered the mosquitos. They buzzed in his ears, landing on his face and did everything they could to bite him. He crawled back inside the tent, working the flap as quickly as he could to keep the flying bloodsuckers out. He lay down again and a mosquito kept buzzing his face. He tried to catch it, but he couldn't.

The sound of the morning horns puzzled Titus and for a few moments he couldn't figure out where he was. Oh yes, the Legion. At least he'd managed some sleep, though he certainly didn't feel rested.

It had been enough days now that everyone knew the routine. Get up, feed and water the mules, pack up the tents, get the wagons in position, pack them, hitch the mules, try and fill your water skin and then gnaw on some hard bread while waiting for things to get moving.

The weather was the same as the previous days. Clear, no clouds, rising dust from the soldiers in front of the Libritors. Carts getting stuck, mules complaining, the smell of shit, sometimes biting flies, men arguing with each other. The paused for lunch and then began marching again for the usual long stretch of time until early evening.

For a while Titus thought. He thought of all the awful things that had happened and when he grew tired of that he just let his head be empty and walked along, just another pair of legs on the big insect called the 47th.

A desperate pounding of hooves on the right side drew everyone's attention. It took a moment for Titus' brain to wake up - and then he wondered if it was the enemy. A shiver of fear coursed threw him. The enemy were horsemen, weren't they? Horse archers and spear throwers and lances. Everyone stopped walking and looked. The 4th cohort was the rear guard again and two centuries immediately came trotting over. No one seemed particularly upset so Titus decided that it was Roman horsemen- the 47th had cavalry- the Ala- for speedy attacks, escorts, scouting, bringing messages and probably other thing Titus didn't know of.

"Shield wall!" one of the 4th cohort centurions called out.

Sedo was there too on his horse. "Sections 9, 10, 11, 12!" he shouted.

Everyone was staring at the optio.

"Move!" Allec said.

Titus looked. Allec was pointing at the Libritor standard, which was upright. *What did that mean again?* He couldn't remember but it didn't matter because Tenax and Glaber and then Alec were pulling the tarp off the wagon and then taking the covers off of the scorpion pieces. Titus ran over and helped Glaber lift the pieces off the wagon and onto the ground where they started to assemble them. Putting them together had been easy before but now the pieces seemed to be shaking. Allec and Tenax had theirs together first and Tenax rushed to the wagon to get a bolt. Finally Glaber and Titus finished but Titus didn't know where it was supposed to be pointing so they just pointed it at the backs of the Legionnaires, the same as the other scorpions. Titus dashed over and grabbed a bolt from the wagon. He tried to put it in the channel but Glaber was shouting at him. They hadn't winched the rope back yet. Titus threw the bolt on the ground and they ratcheted the sinew rope back. Titus picked up the bolt and they were ready to stand by.

"Shields!" Sedo was shouting. "Shields!"

Tenax and Allec rushed to grab their shields from beside the wagon and Glaber and Titus did the same. Glaber slipped and fell in the grass. Titus sat his shield on the ground, angled it and crouched beside it just like the rest of the Libritors were doing. Glaber was getting to his feet. There were sudden whacks and thuds as arrows landed all around them. Someone in one of the other sections was hit and started screaming. Although the arrows lay thickly Glaber hadn't been hit and he grabbed his shield. Another rain of shafts came down, three thumping into Titus' shield.

All at once, all of the Legionnaires in front of them fell to the ground, like they'd been made of paper and had been knocked over by the wind. Titus was staring over their prone bodies wondering what was going on. Beyond the lying Legionnaires was a mass of horsemen with bows, getting ready to fire again.

Tenax and Allec rushed to their scorpion. Glaber ran to the other one. Titus accidentally looked in the direction of the pennant and saw the red and white material dipping and twirling. Allec and Glaber fired. There was a loud twang and the bolts flew over the prone Legionnaires towards the enemy horsemen, who suddenly started scrambling to get away. They'd released another flight of arrows just before though and they landed all around, some knocking loudly into the wood of the wagon. Both mules from Section XI beside went down screaming painfully. Titus was still looking at the pennant, which had dropped out of sight. Tenax was rushing back for another bolt. Glaber stared at Titus for a moment and then tried to do the winches by himself. Titus grabbed another bolt from the wagon and then threw it down and helped with the winches. Allec fired and the bolt sailed over the crouched Legionnaires towards the retreating horsemen. In the distance a knot of them seemed to stumble and fall. Then the ratcheting was done and Titus put the bolt in the channel. Glaber just stood there.

"Fire it!" Titus yelled. "Shoot!"

He thought maybe Glaber had gone into shock and he pushed the other man out of position and almost fired but stopped when he saw the Legionnaires were all on their feet again. The pennant was back up again, meaning standby. Titus stood by.

Chapter 15

It was done then. That's all there was, their first engagement. The enemy horsemen had ridden close all around the Legion and fired a couple rounds of arrows into the air. The Legion had fired back a handful of scorpion bolts. And then it was time to continue moving.

Titus was exhausted. He was already physically worn out from the days of marching and drilling. He'd been terrified and hyper during the attack and now all of that energy was gone too. There was no time for resting because they'd been ordered to disassemble the scorpions and load them up again. A couple of Legionnaires had come and killed the two wounded mules and then began cutting them up for meat. Titus found the sight shocking.

He was glad XII section's mules hadn't been injured, even though he'd never really thought about them before. A pair of replacement mules were brought up from the baggage train and section XI was ready to go. Soon they were all moving again. Titus was so tired that he had pain in his back and his neck, and a headache. He tried drinking some water but found that his waterskin was empty. He didn't know how that had happened.

There were no further attacks and they marched until evening and then the Legionnaires began to build a marching camp again. The Libritors drilled with swords, pila and shields. For the first time Titus paid attention to the surrounding countryside while they were doing it. The enemy could attack again while the Legionnaires were busy and the Libritors would have to fight them off. The horsemen didn't attack though and soon everyone was safe inside the marching camp. It wasn't really safe though, Titus thought. They could shoot arrows in. Everyone was in danger.

Sedo lectured them while they chewed on their dinner which was dried meet and barley stew.

"You saw your first bit of action," the optio said, frowning. "Four sections fired a few bolts. What did you learn?"

The question hung the air.

"We need to pay attention to the standard," Tenax said loudly and then looked directly at Titus.

"We have to work together," someone in one of the other sections called out.

"We should keep our shields close to the scorpions," someone else suggested.

Sedo nodded affirmatively at each comment. "That wasn't a real attack," he said. "They just wanted to see what we'd do. They were just playing with us."

Playing. Titus wondered how many men had been killed on both sides.

"Stickmen watch the pennant. Markers watch your targets. Don't hit anybody on our side," Sedo said. "Keep your shields nearby. Help each other. Pay attention." Then he walked away.

The Libritors all returned to their tents. Titus hung back. He was ashamed. He knew he'd frozen- that's what they called it. Just stood there, wondering what to do. Wanting to watch the bolts fly through the air and see where they landed. He wondered if Glaber was mad at him. He knew Allec wouldn't be, and also that Tenax definitely was. Those things were to be expected. He didn't know how Glaber felt. He'd liked the young man, felt like they could be good friends. He was too scared to go to the tent. He wandered over to one of the walls.

After today's little attack, the watch was being more careful. Several soldiers stood together, shields up, almost making miniature testudos. They peeked out. The number of Legionnaires on watch had doubled. They smiled at Titus.

"You're a Libritor, aren't you?" one of the Legionnaires asked.

Titus nodded, embarrassed.

"Nice shooting today! I heard you got a couple of those bastards!"

Titus kept walking. He went to the area were the mules were tethered and sat down with them. It smelled bad, but he figured it was okay because he felt like shit.

"Titus?"

He looked up. Glaber was looking for him. The other man had never gotten in the habit of calling Titus by the cognomen they'd given him- Ramuscalus. Titus didn't answer but the other man found him anyway.

"Everybody makes mistakes," Glaber said. "Don't be so hard on yourself."

"I was useless."

"You had to learn somehow. Next time you'll do better." He held out his hand, which was wrapped in a bandage. "I broke my finger. I was so nervous I did something when we were ratcheting. It hurts."

"I will do better," Titus said. "Thanks for looking for me."

"I thought maybe you were out somewhere thinking about your girl."

Titus made a face. "What girl?" *Did Glaber know about Elonia?*

"Back at Dertona, you said you gave money to a girl. I thought you must have meant your girlfriend," Glaber said.

Titus shook his head. "That's done. I have no girlfriend."

Glaber punched him playfully on the shoulder. "No shame," he said. "Neither do I."

The two men went back to the XII section tent. The camp was

much noisier than normal and more soldiers were still up, dicing, talking or milling around.

"I think everyone's on edge," Glaber said. "We'll probably get attacked again tomorrow."

Allec was still up, singing to himself. Tenax was also awake, frowning in the lamplight.

Titus felt that he had to apologize. "I'm sorry for what happened today. I will do better."

Allec stopped his singing and Tenax looking at him.

"What are you talking about?" Tenax said.

"In the fight. I didn't know what to do."

Tenax laughed. He actually laughed. "I put the bolt in backwards the first time," he said. "I never even noticed what you did."

Chapter 16

Is it possible that a person can only get so tired and no more? Titus awoke to the horns, as usual. He climbed out of the tent with everyone else. He didn't feel that awful. Maybe it was relief- he'd survived their first engagement. He'd do better. He'd done so badly that it was probably impossible to repeat.

The march began. Trampled grass, dust, ruts, blue sky filled with haze. Hills around. No sign of the enemy. They did something unusual when they stopped for lunch. They'd halted later than usual. Titus guessed it was because the legate wanted them to be on top of a small hill that had a good lookout of the surrounds. He didn't care about the view, he just wanted to rest and eat. The horns never sounded the get ready to march.

"What's happening?" Titus said.

The rest of section XII looked at him.

"We're not doing anything," Titus continued.

Glaber laughed. Tenax shook his head.

"Don't complain," Allec said. "Rest." He closed his eyes and began singing softly to himself.

Glaber and Tenax reclined and closed their eyes. Titus had noticed Sedo coming towards them. He was walking easily, like he had in the old days before things had gotten so serious.

Titus stood and saluted and the optio waved at him to sit down again. Sedo took a seat beside Titus.

"XII section," Sedo said quietly.

Glaber and Tenax opened their eyes and sat up. Allec was softly snoring. Tenax nudged the veteran with his boot and Allec startled awake.

"Now that we're all here," Sedo began with a smile, "I can give you your new orders. First, you're to prepare the scorpions for transport."

"They're already on the wagon," Glaber said.

Sedo held up a hand for silence. "By horse. So make sure all the parts are secure, that the covers will keep them dry and clean and that they can be tied onto a horse."

"What's happening?" Tenax asked.

Sedo smiled again. "I believe the Legate has sent up his pavilion. You're to report there for your orders. Good luck." He rose and went over to Section XI, where he began saying the same sort of thing.

They unloaded the scorpion's pieces from the wagon and made sure they were tightly covered and secure. Then Allec led the way through the resting Legion to the Legate's pavilion, which had been erected in the centre of the soldiers.

Titus' knees were shaking and he wasn't sure why. They were going to be doing something and he was afraid. He glanced at his section mates; Tenax looked like he was thinking about something serious, Allec was busy looking around and humming and Glaber appeared as terrified as Titus felt.

The Legate's guards bade them sit and they waited until the Libritors from Sections 9, 10 and 11 arrived. Five cavalry decurions arrived, recognizable by their metal greaves and long cavalry swords. A tribune was with them. After about twenty minutes the Libritors were invited into the pavilion.

There were sixteen Libritors so even though the pavilion was large, space was tight. They were told not to salute even though they were surrounded by officers. The 47th 's Gold Eagle standard was displayed against one wall of the red pavillion. Titus had never seen it before and hadn't expected to be impressed by it. Its gold shone, the eagle was sculpted with wings outstretched and lightning bolts gripped by the bird's talons.

"Company at ease!" a man snapped.

Everyone stood at ease. Titus leaned over a little so he could see who was talking. There were four men standing at the front, all without helmets. One Titus recognized as First Spear Castus, the highest centurion in the Legion. He was the one who'd ordered them to stand *at ease*. Beside Castus the three others wore the breastplates of tribunes.

"Welcome all," a new voice spoke. "I'm Legate Marcus Lavinius Horatio. Beside me are our senior tribune, Marcus Linneaus Politio, and the commander of the Ala, Tribune Gaius Cestro Nimmenus. You're probably wondering why you've been summoned here." The Legate paused to lick his lips. "No, you're not in trouble."

Everyone laughed politely.

"One of our challenges in fighting the Ozani is that they refuse to be pinned down. They're happy to scamper around all day on their little ponies. Our intelligence reports that the force causing the trouble is led by the two largest clans. They are lead by two leaders, one from each clan, because a clan won't take orders from someone not in their clan. So if we can't bring them to battle we've got to defeat them some other way. You, Libritors, are now assassins. With the help of the Ala, we're going to transport you to the Ozani camp and under cover of darkness you will fire as many bolts as you can into the clan leaders' tents. Hopefully we'll kill both of them, or one of them or even just scare them enough so that they give up and go home. Their army is made of several clans, and if their current leadership fails, they will resort to fighting each other instead of us." The Legate held his hand up for emphasis. "This is not a suicide mission. I'm expecting you to return. We must be fast and deadly. Above all we must be vigilant, to see our best chance and seize it when the moment is ripe."

The officers politely applauded the word vigilant, as it was the 47th's nickname: *Vigilianti.*

The Legate continued. "Each section of Libritors will be accompanied and protected by one turma of cavalry. You can trust the Ala to get you home."

Senior tribune Politio spoke next. He was an older man, rumoured to be a distant relative of the current emperor, which is probably why he was far from Rome at this moment.

"You may not have opportunity to bring your scorpions back with you. If that's the case, you must destroy them before leaving them."

"Any questions?" the Legate asked.

There were none. For some reason, Titus had a metallic taste in his mouth. *Was that the taste of fear?*

They were dismissed. As they exited the pavilion they heard the third tribune, the one in charge of the Ala, asking the Legate why he was not being allowed to go on the mission. They returned to their tents where they met up with Praedirus, Decurion of the thirty troopers of Umbra squadron.

The Decurion had the Libritors remove their mail armor and anything else that might make noise. Section XII was issued with extra food and water rations and told to wait until night.

Chapter 17

The Legion rested until dusk, then it prepared to move again. Generally they didn't move at night. The hope was it would distract and mask the movements of the Ala carrying the scorpions. The enemy was probably used to the Ala coming and going for they functioned as the 47th's scouts. The trick was going to be creating enough of a diversion so that the some of the Ala could slip away unnoticed into the night.

The Legate had chosen his night well. It was the night of Argolath- one of three times during the year when there would be no moons. The grassland weather was usually clear so the stars would still be out. It was the best that could be done.

Praedirus, decurion of Umbra squadron, came and supervised the loading of the scorpions. Umbra was taking section XII and two horses were assigned to carry both a trooper and a scorpion. Four horses would be carrying a trooper and a Libritor; necessary because none of the Libritors were competent horsemen. Four more troopers would be accompanying to assist- a total of ten riders.

Titus was nervous. He'd been permitted to bring his sword,

nothing else. No helmet, no chain mail, no shield. The Ala was providing food and water. While they waited for the horns XII darkened their faces and hands with dirt and ash.

The enemy must have wondered what the 47th was doing. Instead of marching all day they had rested all afternoon and evening. Now that it was sunset the horns were blowing and the Legionnaires were getting on their feet to move. Maybe the enemy wasn't curious- after all they'd avoided confronting the Legion. They probably thought that this was some new tactic, moving at night.

Everyone began marching. All thirty troopers of Umbra squadron rode off- including the ten with the special mission. They took their time, so they didn't tire the double-loaded horses. Titus had learned the name of the trooper he was riding behind. Carro was twenty-three and smiled easily. He tried to put Titus at ease and told him he was going to have to hold on to his back while they were moving.

Titus just nodded and said yes to everything. It was eerie being away from the column. He'd felt safe with 5000 Legionnaires around him. Now there were just thirty troopers and section XII. He was holding on to Carro's back but Titus knew if they were going faster he'd probably fall off.

Umbra squadron rode at an easy pace for a bit, then split into three groups of ten. The enemy was probably watching; however all four turmae were doing the same thing so now the enemy scouts would have to watch twelve groups of riders. Hopefully one would be able to get the job done.

Soon it was just the ten of them riding in the starlight. Still they were taking their time. Carro had explained that night patrols were dangerous because you couldn't see the holes- the grassland was inhabited by some kind of small rat like animal that dug a lot of holes. A misstep could break a horse's leg, and doom its rider to be left behind.

The longer they rode the tighter Titus held onto Carro. The trooper smelled like sweat and leather, since he wore no metal armour as ordered. The horse smelled too, like a horse. Titus wondered if it had a name. The Libritors hadn't named the mules. Well, they'd called them section XII. Titus realized he was silly with lack of sleep and the constant riding motion. He'd tried to sleep in the afternoon like everybody else but he'd been too tense. Now he felt too relaxed, like jelly, waited to drop off the horse and disappear down a rat hole.

Carro was poking at Titus; Titus must have fallen asleep. They'd stopped moving.

"Can you get down?" Carro asked quietly.

Titus was still holding onto Carro. His fingers were stiff because he'd been gripping tightly for so long. Also he wasn't sure how to get off. He couldn't swing his leg over in front of him because Carro was sitting there. He felt a tap on his leg- it was Glaber and another trooper, their arms open. Titus let himself fall into their embrace as his far leg slid off the horse. He was standing then, his legs wobbly. He felt for a moment that he might throw up but the feeling quickly passed.

Decurion Praedirus had stayed with them. Three of the troopers were on lookout; the rest, along with the four Libritors gathered around the Decurion. Titus noticed that they were in small valley- he didn't know what else to call it. It was not big. They were in the middle of three hills and the so-called valley between them dipped enough so that the men and horses were out of sight.

"No fire, no loud noise, no going up the hill," Praedirus said. He had a gruff way of speaking and a puckered scar so big on one side of his face that it was easily visible in the starlight.

"First," the decurion continued, "unload the scorpions from the horses. Then you can eat and sleep."

The sleeping part greatly appealed to XII section and they quickly assisted the troopers in getting the wrapped pieces of equipment off the horses. Then Tenax, Allec, Glaber and Titus all lay down close together, as if they were still in their tent- force of habit. Now that they'd stopped moving the mosquitos began to buzz them. Titus put his scarf over his face and fell asleep despite the buzzing.

When he awoke the sun was already up in the sky. The horses were calmly munching on the grass- some of it was even greenish in the little valley. Others were sleeping or sitting. Everyone looked like they'd just rolled in the dirt, because their faces were still covered in mud and ash.

Glaber was already awake. He looked like he was

daydreaming.

"What are you thinking about?" Titus asked, surprising the other young man.

For a moment Glaber looked like he wasn't going to answer but then he frowned. "Home," he said.

"Did you live in the town?" Titus asked.

"A small farm. Just my father and I." His face darkened. "I'm sorry- I shouldn't have mentioned my father."

"Why?"

"Because I didn't want to make you think of yours."

Titus gave a small nod and looked away. His gaze fell on Tenax, who had taken his boots off and was rubbing his feet. He had ugly feet.

"Why did you join the Legion?" Titus asked, turning back.

Glaber shrugged. "It was the lesser of many bad things."

"I'm sorry," Titus said.

Glaber shrugged again.

One of the lookouts up on the hill made a small noise and all the troopers reacted. Three went to the horses to keep them calm and quiet. The Decurion whispered to the Libritors.

"There is an enemy patrol nearby, so you must be absolutely quiet. They can't see us, but their horses may be able to smell us. And horses' ears are very good."

The Libritors fell silent. Unbelievably, Titus felt a sudden urge to sneeze. He buried his face in his scarf and lay on his stomach, pressing his face into the ground.

Chapter 18

They passed the entire day in the valley. Titus found it difficult to sleep even though he was tired. It wasn't just that it was daylight; the air seemed full of tension too. It was like they were playing a game of hide and find but with swords. It was also boring. There was little to do and Praedirus hadn't given them permission to speak after the patrol had passed. It was probably fine by now. He just hadn't gotten around to it.

At sunset they had another meal and began loading up the

horses again. The horses were patient and calm. Probably they'd picked the best ones for this mission. Titus thought back to the meeting with the Legate, when he stressed this wasn't a suicide mission. *How was that possible?* A group of ten confronting the entire enemy army? The Legate had said that so that they wouldn't refuse to go. Would it really make that much of a difference if the enemy leader was killed? Were they that different than Romans? If the Legate died the senior Tribune would simply take over. It was mind-blowing to think that the world was so different everywhere.

As soon as it was fully dark they set out. They had split up into groups of three now, and a couple of the troopers were out scouting ahead. Titus was riding with Carro again. Just like the night before, they were travelling safely rather than quickly.

"Do we even know where the enemy camp is?" Titus whispered to Carro.

"Yes," the trooper said quietly.

The moons were peeking out tonight, just slivers of them. To Titus' eyes, the world seemed vast, endless and empty, if you didn't count the grass.

The three horses of Titus' group stopped. One horse carried the scorpion and a trooper, Glaber and a trooper were on the second. Every one dismounted – again they helped Titus off- and they began walking with the horses.

"We're getting close now," Carro whispered.

Decurion Praedirus appeared out of the grass, his horse no where in sight.

"Libritors with me," the decurion said.

The troopers stayed with the mounts. The Libritors and Praedirus walked for a few more minutes and then it was down on all fours crawling. It was easy for the first little bit but it quickly became tiring. They began to go slower and slower and Titus wasn't sure if it was because Praedirus was tried or because they were getting closer to their objective.

Finally, they were on the side of a grassy hill. Praedirus dropped to his stomach and motioned for them to do the same. They wiggled the last of it, and then came to the hill's crest. Below them, shadowing in the starlight, was the enemy camp. It was immense. Not organized like a Roman marching camp was. There were tents everywhere, with horses tethered outside the tents.

There seemed to be no roads or path, just haphazard tents. They could see the men on guard duty. They were on horseback, riding along the edge of the camp. The breeze smelled of cook fires and excrement.

"How long do you need to setup?" Praedirus asked. "It will take us an hour to haul the scorpions to this spot. How much time after that?"

"Half an hour," Glaber said.

Praedirus nodded.

Titus was peering at the camp, at the dark tents trying to see if one of them stood out. He couldn't see their colours in the night, so he was trying to judge by size. It was difficult because the camp was so big and the tents further away seemed identical. Glaber elbowed him sharply in the ribs.

"There," Glaber was pointing. "Do you see it?"

After a moment, Titus did. A bigger tent, surrounded by smaller ones. It looked like there were flags and pennants there too but it was hard to tell in the dark.

"Are they in range?" Titus asked.

Glaber seemed to be thinking about it. "Maybe," he said. "Allec would be the better judge."

Titus wondered where the rest of section XII was. There was a sound behind them and Praedirus' head poked out from the grass.

"Get your butts over here and help us!" he snapped angrily.

Glaber and Titus scrambled down the hillside on their bellies as quickly as they could. The Decurion was furious.

"Did you think you were going to sit around while we moved the fucking scorpions for you?" he growled.

"Sorry, sir," Glaber said. "We were checking for the best target."

The statement seemed to quiet the Decurion and Titus was impressed. He wouldn't have dared to talk back to him.

When they arrived back at the horses, Carro and the other troopers had already unloaded the scorpions. Allec and Tenax and their scorpion were there too, along with all of the other troopers.

"Did you see a leader tent?" Allec asked.

Glaber nodded. "The range is extreme. I'll need your help in aiming."

Allec nodded. Tenax didn't say anything.

They spent the next hour hauling the scorpions through the grass and up the hill. Praedirus and the troopers helped. After some discussion, they decided to assemble the artillery pieces on the side of the hill and then everyone would work together to get them up to the top where they could fire.

Titus could have assembled the scorpion with his eyes closed. He found it more difficult when his hands were shaking. When both units were ready they carried them up on top of the hill. Praedirus brought up an armload of bolts. The horses and all the troopers now waited directly behind the small hill.

"How many shots do you think we'll have time for?" Tenax asked.

"None if we don't get to it!" Allec said.

Both teams cranked their scorpions back. Allec quickly adjusted his aim, lowering the back end and raising the front to give the bolt more height and hopefully greater reach. He trotted over and helped Glaber do the same. Tenax and Titus fitted the bolts into the channels.

Allec didn't delay, he immediately fired. Glaber quickly did the same. The scorpions made a loud thudding *thwang* sound as the bolts disappeared into the night.

Chapter 19

"Reload!" Glaber shouted at Titus.

He'd been staring into the darkness at their target.

"There's no time, reload!" Glaber shouted again.

Titus could hear the sound of Tenax and Allec ratcheting their scorpion back to fire again. He rushed to help Glaber do the same. Tenax had put another bolt in the channel and Allec fired. Titus grabbed a bolt and loaded the weapon. Glaber fired and they began ratcheting back again.

"Keep firing!" Praedirus ordered. "I'll tell you when to stop!"

Titus focused on cranking and loading the bolt. A trooper came with another armful. They'd each fired three times now. Titus wanted to look at the camp. He stole a long glance as he grabbed a bolt and brought it back to the scorpion. He couldn't really see anything in the dark, and they were making too much noise to hear anything.

"Faster!" Praedirus urged.

Both scorpions fired again. They ratcheted them back and Tenax and Titus ran for another bolt.

"Last shot!" Praedirus snapped.

They both fired and Titus had a chance to see what was happening in the enemy camp. There were two things to see- the camp, which now looked like an ant hill that someone had kicked because everything was moving; and much closer, a line of horseman riding angrily at them.

"Get to the horses," Praedirus ordered. He had a hammer in his hand.

"I'll take that!" Tenax grabbed it from the decurion. "I know the scorpions better than you do- I'll make sure they're useless- go, I'll catch up!"

Everyone was running down the hill to the horses. The troopers were already mounted, the horses prancing, ready to go. Carro pulled Titus up and they began to ride. Titus glanced back and saw Praedirus waiting for Tenax, who could still be seen on the top of the hill. Suddenly there were other shapes on the hill top, dark silhouettes in front of the stars. Praedirus spurred his horse and galloped after the troopers. The dark silhouettes flowed over the hill and gave chase.

It was quickly apparent that the horses carrying two people could not run quickly for very long. Praedirus had quickly caught up and the other troopers rode closer in a tight group.

"Closer!" Praedirus ordered. "Closer!"

The horsemen rode even closer together. Behind them, their enemies began to shoot. An arrow whizzed past Titus's head. Another hit the trooper in front. The man cried out and fell out of the saddle.

"Stay together!" Praeirus screeched. He could barely be heard above the pounding of the horses. "Closer!"

Titus began to panic. Was the decurion trying to get them all killed? If they stayed close together they were an easy target. He gripped Carro's shoulders more tightly. He could shout at Carro, or he could try to fall off, though he'd probably be injured or killed and likely trampled by the other horses in the close group. Titus turned his head and looked behind. They were moving around so much it was hard to see but it seemed like the enemy was gaining on them. As he looked an arrow cut past his face, slicing a line of pain into his right cheek. The trooper on the next horse in front of them took the arrow in the back of the neck and fell. The horses trampled him and kept going.

Then Titus heard the familiar twang of a scorpion. And then another and another. He looked behind again and the pursuing riders were stopping and turning around. Another scorpion fired and hit an enemy horse and threw into some other riders. The scorpions continued firing even though the enemy was now racing the other way.

Carro and the other troopers reined in their horses and slowed them. They'd been running full out for several minutes, some with two riders. The animals breathed heavily and so did the riders. Glaber threw up.

Allec looked around. "Where's Tenax?"

Praedirus shook his head. "He never made it."

There was no time to waste. Section X and section XI packed up their scorpions and rode off. The three empty horses, who'd been trained to keep up even if their trooper fell, we're put to work carrying the scorpions.

"Faster!" Praedirus ordered! "They will be upon us!"

The Libritors and troopers jumped on their mounts and the group started off again. They rode a short ways and met up with section IX, who'd was covering the retreat. The enemy were still following, but at a great distance. The troopers started to relax. Titus felt Carro calm and stretch and that relaxed Titus too.

The sun began to rise. Some of the Libritors from the other sections were waving their arms and celebrating. All four turmae of Ala were together now, riding back to the camp.

For a moment Titus felt joy – he'd survived. They'd accomplished their mission, though he had no idea if they'd hit any of the enemy leaders. They'd given them something to think about, at any rate. Tenax was gone, either dead or captured. Titus had mixed feelings about that. Section XII had been a team, and he'd miss that. Tenax was also the man who'd killed his father. In self defense. And Tenax was possibly a spy. Titus sighed-so much confusion. Anyway all that was finished now.

Section XII had also left behind their scorpions. Tenax had stayed to damage them and make them useless to the enemy. Titus wondered if he, Glaber and Allec would be put in with the Legionnaires now. He shook the thought away. That made no sense. They weren't fighters. They were Libritors.

The Ala and its guest riders grew wearier as the day wore on. It was hot but they didn't stop for water or to eat. At some point Titus became aware that there was more horseman ahead. It turned out they were the rest of the Ala, the ones that had stayed with the 47th. They'd come to welcome their comrades home.

Soon it was in sight. The 47th had built a marching camp. Titus had never been so happy to see something in his life. The walls, ditches, towers and regular rows of tents looked like home.

Chapter 20

The camp was in a joyous mood. The general feeling was that they'd struck a powerful blow against the enemy. Allec, Glaber and Titus stayed in their tent. They weren't feeling the joy. They were tired, and they'd lost Tenax and both their scorpions.

Optio Sedo threw open the front flap without warning.

"It sounds like you did great!" he congratulated them and handed Glaber a wine skin. "A little celebratory gift," he said with a smile.

They nodded.

He stepped into the tent, sat down with them. "The Legion is a strange job," he said. "When there's no fighting, it's boring and everyone wishes for action. When there's a war everyone dreads the fighting and wishes for peace. You may have done terrible things and maybe terrible things were done to you. You lost a comrade. But you're alive today, and that's what you must celebrate. Think- it might have been you who didn't return. Or maybe that little attack has changed the course of history. Maybe the Ozani will pack it up and go home, saving thousands of lives. Or maybe they'll focus on us, instead of raiding settlements. Whatever you choose to think your actions changed things. For whatever sacrifices were made, we hope dividends are paid. Don't think that you're paid to kill others. You're paid to keep the Roman peace, so that all may flourish."

Titus realized that Sedo was drunk. The Optio produced another wine skin and held it high.

"To peace and war!"

Glaber took a swig from the wineskin and passed it to Allec. The older man took a rather substantial drink before handing it to Titus. Titus swallowed a mouthful. It was good wine.

"The Legate has asked to see the sections who went out this evening," Sedo said. "I expect we'll be getting a decoration for our sorry standard. Make sure your uniform is smart," Sedo advised. "I'll gather you little birds at sunset."

Allec had taken the wineskin and was drinking what was left. He wiped his mouth with his forearm.

"You boys don't realize how great a thing we did," the older man said. He drank the rest of the wine. "We all die some time; be happy it wasn't your turn." He laid back, closed his eyes and began singing softly to himself.

Glaber and Titus slipped out of the tent. It was late afternoon and they could have done anything but they didn't feel like it. Eventually they made their way to the turf wall.

The Legionnaires there asked if the young men had been the Libritors who'd went on the mission. They were congratulated, slapped on the back, and offered wine. As much as they were determined to be glum it did help raise their spirits.

"It's funny," Glaber said when they were alone, "I left home to have adventure and success. And now all I can think about is some of the quiet and peaceful times on the farm." He smiled. "I'd probably last a whole afternoon before I wanted to leave again."

Titus laughed a little because that's what was expected of him. He too felt out of sorts. He didn't want to go home. But this didn't seem right either. It was like he'd discovered a new version of himself and he really didn't know what to do with it.

They spent some time cleaning their uniforms and dressing. One good thing about not having taken the chain mail with them on the mission was that he hadn't gotten dirty. They woke Allec, who was still asleep. It was almost sunset.

Optio Sedo, was looking bright and sparkly and even more drunk, when hecame and gathered the four sections who'd been on the mission. They received a few cheers as they marched to the Legate's big pavilion tent, the sky orange behind it.

This time there was more room inside and they were allowed to sit down. No one from the Ala was there- they'd already had their own ceremony. Legate Marcus Lavinius Horatio and the Senior Tribune Marcus Linnaeus Politio congratulated them all and presented Optio Sedo with a silver Phalera- a decorated disk that would be added to the scorpion Libritor standard. The Phalera had an eye for the 47th, and the date carved into it. First Spear Castus was in attendance too, ordering slaves to and fro as they served wine and food by the bright light of many lanterns.

Allec was laughing and drinking as much as he could. Titus was eating the chicken- actual fresh chicken- and Glaber was secretly swiping some of the bread and hiding it in his tunic. It was, Titus thought, one of the best times he'd had in recent memory. And then everything came crashing down.

So many things happened at once. There was the sound of the leather tent ripping, a scream as a serving slave's torso exploded in a splash of blood and flesh and a crack as one of the wooden tent poles broke. The tent began to fall and caught fire from some of the smashed lanterns. The last thing Titus saw was the Legate staggering and falling with a scorpion bolt through his stomach.

There were screams and shouts and flames. Under the tent people were fighting, trying to crawl past each other by scraping, scratching and punching. The loud voice of First Spear Castus cut through everything.

"ATTENTION!" he screeched. "UNDER THE TENT ATTENTION!"

Most of the struggling Libritors froze in place.

"Legionnaires cut through the tent and get them out.!" Castus ordered.

Titus felt the cool air as part of the tent was lifted and cut open. The flames responded to the influx of fresh air too, leaping and burning. A pair of strong hands grabbed at Titus and began to drag him. He quickly began to crawl on his own and the hands released him and went back for someone else.

It was a shock when his head popped out into the cool night air. Those coming out of the collapsed burning pavilion were urged to stand nearby. Titus stumbled over, coughing.

All around the camp was in movement. There were easily two hundred Legionnaires working at the Legate's downed pavilion. Some were beating the flames while others were pulling out those trapped inside. Beyond that bright fire Legionnaires were forming up and the horns were sounding everywhere.

Titus was scraped and cut but that was all. Mostly he was stunned. The enemy had killed their leader with scorpions.

Chapter 21

Life in camp changed from a place of safety and rest to one of terror. All through the night flaming arrows arced through the sky, landing amongst the tents and wagons, starting fires and terrorizing animals. Scorpion bolts tore random paths through tents and supplies. For a while they targeted the four corner towers, knocking Legionnaires off and smashing the wood. Most of the soldiers were ordered against the walls where at least there was some protection from the onslaught.

Glaber and Titus huddled against one of the walls, their shields leaned above their heads. They had the perfect view to watch the mayhem. Optio Sedo had crept by earlier, telling them to sit tight. Anyone poking their head or scorpion up would likely die a quick death. Senior Tribune Politio, who was now in charge of the 47th since the Legate was dead, had ordered everyone to hunker down and wait out the storm of arrows and bolts.

Titus looked over at the burning tents of the hospital section. The wounded had all been dragged outside to bleed under the stars. Allec was one of them; he'd been badly burned in the flames of the Legate's pavilion tent. Titus was upset. He couldn't stop thinking about Tenax. Now he was certain that Tenax had been a traitor. They'd heard that the enemy horsemen had no artillery- Tenax must have just stood on the hill and waited for them to arrive. This was all Tenax's doing. Titus sat shivering, his arms hugging his legs, dreaming of the ways he'd kill Tenax when next they met.

"Titus," Glaber whispered. "Can I tell you something? Titus?"

"Sorry, I must have dosed off. What were you saying?"

Glaber was silent.

"Glaber, what were you saying?"

Titus turned and looked at his comrade. Glaber was staring at him, his eyes large and brown, reflecting some of the flames of the nearby burning tents.

Glaber was quiet for several moments and then asked," Titus what are you thinking about?"

"Killing Tenax. He gave our scorpions to the enemy."

Glaber's face changed. "This is more than two scorpions, Titus. There's at least two firing on each side. Maybe more than ten total."

Titus turned away. "I still think Tenax is at the bottom of this." He swatted at a mosquito.

You wouldn't think that a person could sleep amidst such an attack, but many did. Titus and Glaber eventually succumbed. When Titus opened his eyes he was lying on the ground, curled up under his shield. It was light. He peeked out. It was early morning. Besides the Legionnaires on watch, most everyone else was asleep, huddled against the wall and under shields. It was strangely quiet. Titus realized it was because the arrows and bolts had stopped.

The camp was a sorry sight. Almost all of the tents were down. Those that weren't burned had been trampled or knocked over. Mules were wandering and grazing everywhere. And there were bodies. There was a Legionnaire that had been spitted by a scorpion bolt. His neck was bent back at an impossible angle. His eyes were still open; dead eyes, staring at nothing. His mouth wide, as if he'd died in the middle of a scream. And there were more.

A horn blew a familiar tune. Summons to breakfast. Glaber peeked out from under his shield. Titus was incredulous. Had the bucinator gone mad and just blown whatever he could find in his head? The tramping of boots and the clink of metal and armour drew the attention of both Libritors. A neatly formed column of Legionnaires was marching along the wall. The Senior Tribune, resplendent in his bronze breast plate, was at their head. They were marching twenty steps and stopping. Then repeating.

The Senior Tribune held his hand up and stopped the column when they were close to Titus and Glaber.

"Friends," the Senior Tribune called out. "Legionnaires. The attack is over. The cowards were too afraid to come to our turf walls. It's safe to stand and move around." He opened his arms wide, as if to highlight the lack of projectiles hitting him. "Let us share breakfast, and then we'll start making them pay for this." Tribune Politio smiled broadly. His teeth were yellowy and long, like an old horse's.

Despite everything that had happened, Titus found himself smiling back.

"Yes!" he called out, and let out a cheer.

He was surprised to hear that he wasn't the only one. The Senior Tribune nodded and continued on another twenty steps and gave the same speech. He was travelling the perimeter of the wall speaking to every Legionnaire and soldier.

Everyone stood. Glaber and Titus joined them. They walked back to their flattened tent through the chaos and had breakfast. They didn't know what to do after that so they went to the hospital area. All the patients were still outside because all of the hospital tents had burned. They found Allec. Half of him was oozing yellow pus over the cracked blackened skin. He was delirious. He was busy singing to himself. At least that hadn't changed.

They checked on the Section XII mules. All of the Libritor mules were still tethered. Several were dead. It had been the baggage mules that had gotten loose.

All in all, in no longer seemed as hopeless as it had last night. A lot of the tents were ruined, but the nights were clear and dry. There were going to be mosquitos, but they could survive that.

Sedo came by with the good news that he had a scorpion for them. The bad news was that everyone in Section X had died last night. Sedo gathered all the Libritors together and they shared equipment. Titus and Glaber still had their tent. The poles were broken, but they could fix that or find something. Sedo didn't know what was going to happen next. He told the Libritors everything he knew. The enemy had gathered around them in a huge circle. They were out of scorpion range at this time, but the ballista and onager crews were setting up. Two cohorts of Legionnaires had been tasked with cutting more turf to reinforce the walls and make them higher. They were going to make some turf structures within the camp as well.

"Are we staying here?" Titus whispered to Glaber. "I thought we were going to attack."

Glaber shrugged. "If we go out the gate the horsemen will charge us, or back off. Pepper us with arrows and bolts. They're not going to stand and fight us."

Titus didn't say anything in reply. *How were they going to get out of this?*

Chapter 22

"You crank it like this," Sedo was trying to explain. He was on his knees, underneath the scorpion.

The turf walls had been thickened and heighten. They were taller than a man now. Each wall contained platforms for the scorpions. The wall dipped in the spot where they'd shoot. Unfortunately that left the Libritors open to return fire.

"Keep everything below the wall. They won't see you ratcheting- they'll only see big movements, or your heads. If you stick your head up there, it will get ripped off. Remember there's archers out there too looking for targets."

The Libritors watched silently. The past several days had been hard on everyone. The days for the most part had been quiet, and they'd used them to reinforce their walls. Every night was the same- fire arrows and scorpion bolts. Not as many as the first night, but enough to stop a man from relaxing and sleeping. Causalities, though not many, were adding up. Supplies were dwindling. Already they were eating mule.

"Don't fire unless you've got a specific target," Sedo continued. He didn't need to mention that the were trying to conserve their ammunition.

"How can we target if we don't put our heads above the wall to see?" Mergo from Section VIII asked.

Sedo scowled. "*You* can peek over the wall, Mergo. *You* can stick your whole head up and wave your arms."

There was a little laughter and no more questions.

Titus and Glaber went to the wall position that had been assigned to them. The platform itself was made of sod with wooden boards on top. The boards had come from the wagons. It had been explained that they could easily be reassembled but no one believed that. If they were going to escape there would be no time for wagons.

Initially they'd been issued three bolts. Just three. Then a pair of Legionnaires had stopped by and dropped off twenty more.

"Be ready," they said grimly

Horns sounded and the gates opened on the wall where Section XII was stationed. The gates had been partially smashed by enemy scorpion fire- just to show that they could probably. No enemy had tried to get in.

The smack of studded boots on the hard earth sounded as a thousand men streamed out the gate and formed up in ranks in front of the wall.

Titus and Glaber cranked the scorpion and Titus put a bolt in the channel. Glaber aimed high, above the Legionnaires heads.

Nothing happened.

"Are they just going to stand there?" Titus wondered out loud.

"They're keeping their back to the wall," Glaber said. "If they advance they can be surrounded."

"The enemy's not going to fight us anyway," Titus said.

There were sudden screams as an enemy scorpion bolt tore into the ranks of Legionnaires, killing and maiming.

"Where are they?" Glaber shouted, searching the surrounding landscape with his eyes. "Where are they shooting from?"

The Legionnaires began to quickly advance, as if they were trying to confuse the enemy.

"I don't have anything to shoot at!" Glaber wailed.

Two more enemy scorpion bolts ripped through the Legionnaires, leaving a trail of wrecked red tunic bodies.

Sedo ran by, his face red. "Fire!" he screeched, and kept running.

Glaber fired. At nothing. They couldn't see the enemy anywhere. More bolts were hitting the Legionnaires and they were ordered to retreat back into the camp. Section XII reloaded. There was still nothing to fire at.

The Legionnaires streamed back in through the gate. Another enemy bolt targeted them but fell short, kicking up a cloud of dust and clods of earth. On the other side of the wall the wounded screamed for assistance. For a moment they were ignored. Then a centurion with a single squad of eight ran out the gate. The sight was encouraging until you saw that they were mostly finishing the wounded. Killing them. They brought back only two soldiers, who were able to walk with assistance.

Titus sat back against the wall. He looked at Glaber, who was still looking for a target.

"You should keep your head down or they'll shoot at you," Titus said.

"So?" Glaber snapped. He sounded a little hysterical. He began waving his arms in the air. "Shoot me you fuckers!"

Nothing happened. Glaber grew tired of being an ignored target and finally gave up, collapsing against the wall beside Titus.

That night they had roasted mule for dinner. It was a little tough, but filling. After darkness fell a century of Legionnaires wearing no armor, their faces and exposed flesh blackened, snuck out of the camp. Titus and Glaber watched them go from their scorpion position.

"I hope they're going for the enemy scorpions," Glaber said.

"I hope they're going for help," Titus said without enthusiasm.

The night was the same as the previous ones. A couple rounds of fire arrows and scorpion bolts flew in, spread out so there was not chance to get a good sleep between them. Near Section XII a man began to cry. He continued until someone clouted him, the smack sounding loudly through the camp.

• Barley gruel with bits of mule were distributed for breakfast at sunrise. There was no sign of the century of Legionnaires that had snuck out in the night.

"If they don't return that's a good sign," Titus insisted. "It means they've escaped and will get help."

"It means they're all dead," Glaber said. "The horsemen will run them down."

Titus felt his anger rising. "Maybe they're hiding! In a gully! Like we did!" he said loudly.

Glaber's eyes were flashing. "More likely they've grown fucking wings and are now flying around like little owls!"

Titus threw his bowl of gruel, which he'd mostly finished, at Glaber. It hit the other man in his chain mailed chest. Glaber balled his fists.

"Come on!" Titus urged, "Fight me!"

Their loud voices had drawn others, and they grabbed Titus and restrained him. He didn't protest.

"We're all on edge," Mergo from SectioVIII said. "Let's not help the buggers out there by turning on each other."

Titus and Glaber sat a few paces away from each other against the wall. He was still angry. After thinking about it he decided that Glaber's problem was that he was refusing to have hope. Titus recognized that fighting Glaber wouldn't make the other man have hope. It only hurt them both. He didn't hate the other man. The fight reminded him in a way of the fights he'd had with his brothers growing up.

"Glaber," Titus called.

Glaber turned his head to look at Titus. He still looked angry.

"I'm an ass," Titus said. "A sorry ass."

Glaber smiled. "Maybe we'll have you for dinner."

Chapter 23

Around midday the enemy attacked again. It was different this time. Still long range, but no arrows or bolts. A dozen of what looked like melon sized rocks flew into the camp, and bounced and rolled around.

"Great," Glaber said, "now they have a catapult."

The attack was repeated, and although it seemed ineffective, the Legionnaires began to get upset.

Another round of rocks fell from the sky. One hit the ground near Section XII's positon and rolled. Titus and Glaber saw it clearly. It was a head. The Roman helmet still buckled firmly onto the chin. They were shooting back the heads of the century that had snuck out the night before.

There was nothing anyone could do. Just sit and watch the heads bounce and roll. It seemed like only one machine was firing, because it took a while for them to shoot all the heads. They were only doing about ten at a time. After the heads they fired three volleys of severed hands. They finished off with a generous shot of horse shit, though most of it fell short.

That afternoon the rest of the mules were slaughtered and

cooked. Sedo visited all the Libritors at their positions.

He passed a stone hammer to Glaber. "Tonight as soon as it's dark you're to smash the scorpion and break any bolts that you might have. Gather your shield and whatever gear you can carry. We're leaving the camp."

The thought both excited and terrified Titus. He felt some measure of safety in the camp- except that they were running out of food. They'd built the camp around a spring so there was always water, even if it was being rationed. And they were attacked every night. But outside the wall there was nothing to stop the horsemen from riding them down with lances and spears. They'd have only their shields to protect themselves from the relentless arrows, and there would be no hiding from the enemy scorpion bolts.

The rest of the day was subdued. Soldiers were packing up, but they tried not to make a great show of it. The enemy would find out soon enough.

Titus went to the hospital area to visit Allec. Glaber had refused to come. It had made Titus angry again but this time he'd walked away. The medics had been preparing the injured as well. There were a group of them sitting, ready to go. Titus didn't see Allec among them.

"I'm looking for a Libritor named Allec?" he asked one of the medical orderlies.

The man seemed startled by Titus' question. "What did you say?"

"Looking for a Libritor named Allec. He was burned," Titus repeated.

The orderly looked over at a pile dead bodies, and then kept working. Titus didn't go any closer. He didn't need to see Allec's half burnt corpse. He noticed the smell then.

"He's dead," Titus reported back to Glaber.

The other man nodded.

"You knew?"

"We're not marching out Titus," Glaber said. "We're running for our lives. They're not taking anyone who can't walk."

"They... killed him?" Titus said, shocked.

"Maybe," Glaber said. "Better the medics than the enemy."

Supper was lovely roasted mule. Titus had little appetite but he forced himself to eat anyway. That's what everyone was doing. *Eat now, while you have the chance*, they were saying. *It might not come again.*

The daylight dragged on. Almost as if the sun was refusing to leave. The enemy must know, Titus thought. *They must be expecting it. What else can we do?*

Hammers sounded as the sun began to set. Libritors smashed their scorpions. The other artillery crews destroyed the ballistae and onagers. Wagons were wrecked. Extra pila were bent. Over in the hospital area there was a bonfire of all those who wouldn't be coming.

No horns. They didn't want to alert the enemy. The centurions shouted instead. They seemed as loud as the horns. The cohorts were formed singly and then marched out. The Libritors were summoned in the middle. Titus and Glaber fell in line with their shields, pila and swords. They both wore their yokes, with their packs attached.

Optio Sedo was grim and humourless. "Keep up," he warned. "If you fall behind, the enemy will capture you. Torture you. Don't fall behind. If we turn and face them you'll stand as Legionnaires. They'll probably keep us in reserve," he added.

They marched. Through the gates under the stars. Both moons were up and bright. *Why couldn't they have left on Argolath?* There was no chatter amongst the ranks. Everyone was focused on moving. Tensely waiting for the arrows. Titus saw a few dozen horses trot past. It was the remains of the Ala. The Roman cavalry had been steadily depleted through clashes while scouting and horse deaths in the camp.

Pace increased, almost a light run. Just on the edge of panic, Titus thought. He wondered how the walking wounded from the hospital would keep up. A grimmer thought occurred to him. Maybe that was the point. They were probably at the rear. A final distraction to slow the enemy.

They didn't slow. Titus and Glaber were both breathing hard but they kept trotting along. Their shields had grown heavier in their hands. Some bright soul called a quick halt and everyone fastened their shields on to their yokes, still breathing hard.

When they started again the pace was slower. Still fast, but not a trot. Titus didn't look back. He was afraid to see how near they probably still were to the camp. At least they'd be out of range of some of the enemy scorpions, he thought.

They marched all night. Some men fell away. Gave up and sat down as the column marched past. Titus didn't look at them. Tried not to think about them. Struggled not to be one of them.

When the sun began to rise it made Titus giddy. Had they actually been marching all night? There'd been no attack, at least he hadn't heard one. Perhaps they were actually going to get away.

There was a hill in front of them, a glittering hill. The sun was glittering off armor. Heavy cavalry in armor. Facing them. The wide column halted.

On either side there were masses of horsemen. Probably behind them too. They were surrounded.

Chapter 24

They started with arrows. Unending volleys until there was no break between, just arrows landing all around, hitting the shield over your head, slipping past and sinking deep into your thigh or calf or stomach. The 47th didn't stop. The march paused for a moment as shields were snatched off the yoke and then the centurions ordered everyone to keep moving. The centurions kept shouting *faster, faster*! It was probably not so bad at the front of the column but near the back where the Libritors were they were trying not to step on the fallen wounded and failing. You had to keep your shield up because if you didn't the arrows got you. Your shield's protecting the wounded guy on the ground because you're over top of him but they're pushing from behind and you're stumbling and you're stepping in his blood then on his arm and chest and he's given up complaining about it and your eyes meet. His eyes say this will be you and Titus' eyes said I'm sorry, so sorry please just let be get past.

The 47th kept marching at the heavy cavalry on the hill, which was something the cavalry probably wasn't expecting. Who marches towards heavy cavalry? Only those who want to die. But the heavy cavalry began to get concerned- they liked their charge, that unstoppable ramming push, backed by muscular armored horses. If the 47th grew too close the heavy cavalry wouldn't be able to get a good running start. So they charged. They had the bonus of the hill's slope and they rammed into the front ranks of the marching Legion.

Titus couldn't see the charge, but he saw the heavy cavalry begin to move down the slope. He was more worried about the steadily falling arrows. There was half a Legion between him and the heavy cavalry.

He heard a familiar sound and flinched, ducked even before his mind put the word scorpion in his head. The enemy scorpions were on a hill the left side; he could see them. They were flying a black flag, whatever that meant. They were good, Titus noted. The first shots didn't fall short. Every shot tore into the side of the Legion's ranks.

The heavy cavalry hit the front of the Legion with a crash that was heard all the way back to the rear guard. Then the sound of metal hitting metal. *Faster, faster,* the centurions ordered, and the optios pushed with their big staffs, unless they were falling, full of arrows.

Titus was running now, barely holding onto the shield. His balance was off because he was holding it above his head. Any misstep would make him fall and there'd be no getting up under the desperate feet behind him. He thought they must be getting close to where the heavy cavalry was ensnarled with the Legionnaires because the arrows and scorpion's bolts were fewer.

A space opened up suddenly in front of him as an enemy rider, covered in iron plates, twirled and struck with a long curved sword, driving the Legionnaires around him back. The wild eyed horse was snorting and kicking and was already bleeding from two or three wounds. Titus could see the enemy's eyes, saw the moment when they looked into his. The rider spurred the horse at Titus, readying the long curved sword to strike.

Titus didn't see an attack. He saw a man and horse trying to escape. So he lunged at the oncoming horse, holding his shield up high with both hands- he hadn't thought to draw his sword and he'd lost the pilum somewhere- he held the shield up high and forced it into the horses face. The horse balked and turned sideways which was perfect for the rider to slash at Titus. But Titus was still pushing, still trying to run with the shield holding it high and the big rectangle of wood and iron came in too fast for the rider and then the horse was moving and they were gone, swallowed into a knot of seething stabbing Legionnaires.

Somehow, Titus was almost at the front of the column. All around him were Legionnaires struggling with the heavy cavalry which had gotten bogged down amongst the shields and pila. Some enemy horsemen had managed to break free and were riding quickly to the sides or back up the hill.

A centurion beside Titus, a broad man as tall as the young Libritor, began shouting "up the hill! Keep going!" But then he was gagging on blood and there was an arrow that looked like it coming out of his mouth. He staggered and fell.

Titus kept going. Up higher on the slope of the hill the Legionnaires were forming lines and he could see the Eagle held high above them. There was another enemy horseman in front of Titus then, this one with some gold plates as well as silver and Legionnaires were rushing at him. The rider swung down with his sword and hacked a chunk out of the Legionnaire in front of Titus. He saw the spray of blood but didn't see the Legionnaire's shield flying through the air until an instant before it hit him in the forehead. He was vaguely aware of some pain coming towards him but he blacked out before the agony hit him.

When he opened his eyes a moment later- he thought it was a moment later- he was on the ground looking up at the sky and it felt like a horse was balanced on his forehead. There was no horse of course and his hand moved to his hairline. His helmet was somehow gone and there was a great swelling. His head was sticky with blood though he wasn't sure if it was his. Probably it was his. He didn't even know how to tell.

As his senses returned it was the quiet that stood out the most. No screaming, no terrified horses and mortally wounded men, no sword on shield or armor. Just a low murmur- people talking. Some moaning.

He moved to sit up and blacked out again. When he opened his eyes- it had only been a moment, hadn't it- the sky overhead was streaked with orange. The sun was setting. Instead of trying to get up this time he slowly turned on his side, to look around. There were people- not soldiers, moving through the field of dead and wounded Romans. He wondered if they were here to help.

Soon he realized that they weren't speaking Latin. They spoke in a harsh, guttural language. They weren't dressed as soldiers but they had weapons. Knives. Long knives. As the sky turned orange above he watched as they worked their way towards him. A short people, with small squinted eyes and broad flat noses. They inspected everybody. If a Roman were wounded, they dragged the soldier to his feet. If the man cried out and fell, they killed him. If the Legionnaire remained standing, they pushed him over to a group of tattered and bloody Romans sitting on the ground. Prisoners. They stripped the dead completely. Boots, armor, tunic, weapons, helmet, everything. They rolled the dead naked bodies into piles so that there was room for the scavengers to walk more easily.

Soon they were at Titus. He was surprised to see that they were women and old men with wispy white beards.

"I'm fine!" Titus screeched as they grabbed at his hands. "I'm fine! I'm fine!"

They pulled him to his feet and a wave of nausea and pain washed over him and he felt himself stumbling. *I can't fall, I can't fall.* He managed to stay on his feet and a woman with a long knife in one hand and baby slung on her back escorted him to where the other prisoner waited.

Chapter 25

No one talked amongst the prisoners. They looked like Titus felt- beaten, exhausted, spent. Titus didn't recognize any of them. Most of them were muscled and broad- Legionnaires, not Libritors, and their faces were muddy and bloody. He plunked himself down on the ground beside a man with an arm wound. He made sure not to bump him.

They sat and waited, watched while the Ozani women and old men processed the dead. The Roman bodies were lumped in small piles. Titus wondered if they were going to bury or burn the corpses. Already crows were circling above, cawing loudly. The Ozani dead were carried carefully off the field, four or more people lifting, like the bodies were fragile wounded men instead of lifeless. The dead horses were cut up for meat.

A string of wagons came along then, and the women and old men began to load them. Swords, armor, shields on one wagon. Carefully wrapped dead horsemen on the next bunch. Then horsemeat, boots, tunics, personal treasures. A bent old man, his face browned by the sun, came with waterskins for the prisoners. They passed them around. The water was very good. It amazed Titus. How can water be so good sometimes and ignorable others? And now when everything seemed awful, the water was so delicious it made him happy. He didn't have any reason to be joyful right now.

Another man stood before the prisoners. He too was tanned from being outdoors, but his features were not Ozani. He was dressed as they were though, with goatskin breeches, and tunic.

"Romans!" he called out in Latin. "I bring you good news!"

"You're setting us free?" a smart Alek Legionnaire quipped.

The man held up a hand for silence. "The Ozani respect warriors. You fought well. Now we will march to their camp. If you fall you will be killed." He smiled. "Don't fall. Come on, on your feet!"

He had a whip with him, which he snapped in the air. Everyone began to stand. Legionnaires were used to discipline. They'd seen the whip. They didn't need to feel it.

Titus actually felt better while walking. It helped to clear his mind, and made the pain in his forehead lessen. Legionnaires with leg wounds were having a much harder time. The others helped them. They all seemed to know each other. Titus knew no one. He walked alone in the crowd.

The camp was much like he'd seen during their scorpion raid, now so long ago. Sprawling, round tents every which way, goats, sheep, people, horses. It smiled like animal dung and smoke. The Romans staggered through it all, grim faced. The Ozani in the camp ignored them.

Titus could see some of the big pavilion tents of the leaders', in the distance. They didn't look damaged at all by scorpion fire. Maybe you could only see it up close.

"Stop!" the man with the whip said.

Everyone stopped.

"Sit."

Everyone did so.

If I'm to be a slave, I should try to enjoy these moments of not working, Titus thought. Or maybe they'll sacrifice us to their gods. If they had gods.

They were fed bowls of warm rice. The rice had green things in it, some kind of mushy leaf. Titus didn't know what it was. Again, he was amazed at how happy eating made him.

While they were eating a large number of horsemen returned to the camp. They were laughing and smiling. They frowned at the captured Romans. Not a good sign.

The wooden bowls were collected and they were given more water. One of the Legionnaires tried to ask where he should go to the bathroom but they ignored him.

After some more time the Latin speaking man with the whip returned, with an Ozani chieftain. It was easy to see the man was one of their leaders. Although he was shorter than the man with the whip he stood very straight with his chin held high. Instead of iron plates for armour, he wore gold. His clothes were trimmed with white fur.

"This is Octar, chief of the Ozani," Mr. Whip announced.

The chieftain took his time looking over the injured Romans. About half, including Titus, met his gaze. Titus tried to imagine what he was thinking. Were they to be slaves? Sacrifices? Dinner?

The chief and Mr. Whip had a long conversation. At the end Mr. Whip bowed and Octar strode imperiously away.

"What's to happen to us?" one of the Legionnaires asked.

"I have good news and bad news," Mr. Whip said.

"Give us the bad news first," one of the Legionnaires called out.

Mr. Whip nodded his head once, agreeing. "You're being gifted to their mercenary allies." Mr. Whip smiled. "That is not good. The good news is that the Ozani have the highest respect for warriors and will not enslave or kill you."

"We're to be set free?" a Legionnaire asked hopefully.

Mr. Whip shook his head. "You're being gifted to their allies, who have no respect for warriors. Or for anyone. That was the bad news, we've already said it. You're going to have to learn to listen." He winked at them, as if he knew some terrible secret that they would soon find out and share.

At sunset Mr. Whip came back with twenty Ozani warriors with spears. They surrounded the Romans. Titus had done a rough count- about fifty Legionnaires. And one Libritor.

"Time to get up!" Mr. Whip shouted, and cracked the whip.

The Legionnaires climbed wearily to their feet.

"March!"

They walked out of the Ozani camp, above them the sky streaked with orange. Another beautiful sunset. At first Titus thought they were just marching out into the grass. Then he saw a small cluster of tents. Ten black tents. There were wagons there too, but no horses. There were scorpions and an onager. A black flag, visible only as a piece of darkness in the orangey sky, flew overhead.

Chapter 26

The Ozani guards marched the wounded Roman prisoners to the black tents and left them sitting there. The man with the whip and the guards returned to the big sprawling Ozani camp. The sun was almost gone now, and the sky was as dark as the two moons and twinkling stars would allow. For a few moments the Legionnaires sat there, then one stood. He waited. All eyes were on him. Everyone knew what he was going to do. There was no one around, no one watching them. The Legionnaire began to slowly move away from the group. After five tentative steps he turned to run... and threw his arms up and fell, a short arrow in his back.

The Romans turned to see a short man- no a dwarf. A real dwarf, about as tall as a human male's chest, with a dark black beard. He was dressed in black and held a crossbow in one hand. He looked like a shadow in the darkness.

"Kannai?" he called out. "Kannai?"

The flaps of one of the black tents parted and another dwarf stepped out. Short and broad, like the one with the crossbow, except he had a white beard instead of black.

"Kannai?" the black bearded dwarf called out again.

"He's asking who's next?" the white dwarf said in Latin.

The Roman prisoners stared at the two dwarves. Titus was thinking what everyone else was. Only two. Dwarves are strong, supposedly, but we are fifty Legionnaires. He hasn't reloaded the crossbow. One Legionnaire at the front stood. The black bearded dwarf produced another loaded crossbow out from behind his back with his free hand.

"Tai kur?"

"He's inviting you to attack him," white beard said.

Perhaps a normal person would have sat. These were Legionnaires, not normal people. Ten more stood. The black bearded dwarf laughed with delight.

"It is a trick," white beard said. "We are all around you. Many weapons. Die now if you wish. For us, it is comic."

It was true. There were dwarves all around them. About fifty, Titus estimated. Most were dressed in colours that blended with the surrounding brown grass. Except for the white beard who'd been speaking Latin to them, they all had black facial hair.

The standing Romans decided to sit down again.

"Dona itben castock vra lauspenchtorq."

"He says don't sit, stand, all," White Beard translated.

Wearily, all the Romans got to their feet.

"This way," White Beard beckoned.

They followed the dwarf. There was a large square hole there, surrounded by tall grasses. Unless you were right upon it, you couldn't see it. It looked to be as deep as a human male. Ten filthy men sat miserably in the hole, staring up at the new arrivals.

"Jump! Go in!" White beard said.

He grabbed the nearest Legionnaire, a man with a leg injury, and forced him into the hole. He landed painfully and cried out. The dirty men already in the hole watched in silence. A couple of Legionnaires immediately lowered themselves in and turned to help the others. Everyone was wounded. In a quick few minutes all the Romans were in the crowded hole.

The Romans took charge immediately. There were no officers but the Legionnaires took care of their own. They designated one corner as the latrine and began to examine the wounds of the injured. The ten previous occupants still sat and watched in silence. Titus stared at them, at their filthy clothes and faces. One of them seemed so familiar. Then he knew.

"Tenax!" Titus called out. "Tenax!" It's me, Titus."

It took a moment for Tenax to understand. It was like his mind was very far away and it took a few moments for him to come back to it. He smiled a little, and then frowned.

Titus took the few steps over. "Tenax. What is this?"

Tenax blinked his bleary eyes. His beard was so full of dust it looked grey instead of black. His face was thin too, like he'd lost a lot of weight. "This is hell, Titus."

"Everyone find a spot to lie down," one of the Legionnaires called out. "We'll come around and check wounds. I'll see if they'll give us some water," the Legionnaire said.

"They won't," Tenax said, but he wasn't speaking loudly. He looked utterly defeated.

Titus sat down beside Tenax. The ten dirty men didn't lie down like the Legionnaires were doing. They sat huddled, close together. Titus wondered if they were doing it for warmth.

"We thought you were dead," Titus said.

"I am," Tenax answered, and then coughed. "I'm just two stupid to realize it yet."

"You've been a prisoner of the dwarves all this time?"

Tenax was silent for a moment. "Not dwarves. They're not dwarves. They're some.... extreme faction. They use us to pull their wagons. To dig. Sometimes they kill us for fun." He licked his dry lips. His tongue looked dry too. "They're mercenaries. Artillery. Scorpions. That's all I know. And that they hate humans."

The hole was silent then, except for the quiet moaning and murmuring of the wounded. Titus managed to lie down and stretch out. The ten stayed sitting. Above, the stars twinkled down. It was a star river night- the two moons were far apart, like the banks of a river, and the stars gleamed like the sparkling water in between.

Chapter 27

Titus slept but it was not good sleep. He dreamt of his father, and of Elonia and both of them were angry and shouting at him.

Tenax was in his dreams too, always standing at the back, almost out of sight, limping, scowling. Then he was dreaming that he was standing on a cliff edge, and the black bearded dwarf pushed him off and he was falling, falling to his death, and then -suddenly awake. His eyes were open and the sky was blue above him. For some reason he noticed the smell first. It wasn't just dirt and sweat and blood and piss- there was something else too. Like rot. He didn't know what it was. His neck was stiff and he moved his aching head slowly, not wanting to cause himself unnecessary pain.

He was of course still in the hole. The prison hole of the dwarven mercenaries. He'd only seen dwarves once before- a travelling troop had come through Dertona. They'd juggled and played instruments and performed crazy balancing acts. He was filled with hate towards the dwarven mercenaries who were holding them captive. Hate so strong he could taste it. He sat up. He was stiff and hungry. Around him the Legionnaires remained lying on the ground. They wouldn't get up until they had to. The ten men who'd been sitting in the pit when they'd arrived were still sitting. Titus looked at them. Dull, empty eyes in dirty faces. Tenax was one of the more aware ones. He turned his head to Titus.

"You didn't die in the night," he said, without malice. "Too bad for you."

"UP! UP!" the white bearded dwarf was urging from the edge of the pit. He had two buckets, which he lowered down. They both held water.

The Legionnaires all began to stir and sit. A pair did not. Their waxen white faces showed them dead or near death. They passed the water around, including the ten sitters. Only seven of them drank, Titus noted.

The white dwarf was back again, throwing chunks of bread this time. If the dwarf had hoped the Legionnaires would fight over it he was disappointed. Soldiers caught the bread and when it had all been thrown they pooled it and divided it. It made Titus proud to be one of them. How could any man betray his brothers?

There was enough bread for every man to have a handful. Titus saw that three of the sitters didn't eat. The ones beside them quickly consumed the untouched bread.

"Now you will climb out!" the white dwarf ordered.

The Legionnaires didn't ask for assistance. One man knelt on his hands and knees and another climbed out. He then lay on the edge of the hole and helped each Legionnaire out of the hole when they were standing on the hands and knees Legionnaire. Another soldier lay down at the top and by the time it was Titus' turn to climb out, near the end, there were many helping hands.

All of the new arrivals were out. They turned to the ten sitters. Beckoned.

Eight of them rose, stiffly. Two stayed sitting. One of the eight- painfully thin- like he was made only of sticks- collapsed down again. All the sitters were skeletally thin. The other seven climbed out with the Legionnaires help. They didn't say thank you.

The dwarven camp had been packed up. The tents were loaded on the wagons, along with the scorpions. These artillery pieces were now bolted onto the wagons, one each. There was a wooden seat at the back of the wagon too, so that a dwarf could sit there and drive the wagon or fire the scorpion. All of the dwarves, about thirty of them, were heavily armed. It looked like some had smeared paste on their exposed flesh- their noses and that little bit around their eyes. Everything else was covered by beard, helmet and armour.

There were no horses or other beasts. The seven sitters took their places in front of the wagons. The long wooden rod coming out, called the tongue, had crossbars on it. They picket up the crossbars and lifted the tongue, ready to go.

"Come on, find a wagon," the white bearded dwarf urged.

The dwarves began to climb onto the wagons. They moved oddly with their short legs and strong torsos.

"Right then," one of the Legionnaires said, "Let's divide up."

Quickly they took spots in front of the wagons. Not all of them carried scorpions. One held a disassembled onager and another three held supplies. When the Legionnaires went to those wagons the dwarves, all of whom seemed to have whips and crossbows, chased them off. The Legionnaires joined other wagons and finally some of the dwarves themselves stood in front of the special four with onager and supplies.

The broad black bearded one who seemed to be their leader

cracked his whip and one of the Legionnaires in front of the scorpion wagon flinched.

"Dunnae!" the dwarf thundered.

The Legionnaires picked up the tongue by the crossbar and began to pull.

"Faster! Faster!" the white-bearded dwarf howled.

It was not as difficult as Titus had imagined. The wagons were well made with extra wide wheels and rolled easily. The land was rolling so going up hill sometimes was difficult. Several times the dwarven drivers hopped down and pushed from the back.

Up and down the hills they went. Off to the right side there was a large dust cloud, and the sound of many horses. The Ozani were on the move too.

Titus wondered where they were going. Since they'd packed up the tents they must be moving camp. He thought of the three men still sitting in the hole. They'd soon be dead like the two Legionnaires who'd died in the night beside them. The whip cracked again. Titus had no sense of direction. There was rolling brown grass in every direction.

After a while he noticed another dust cloud just ahead. They were moving towards it. Probably another group of Ozani, Titus thought.

They came to a hill and strained to pull the wagons up. Dwarves jumped out and pushed from the back, which really helped. The dwarves seemed to be very strong. When they reached the hill top the dwarves cracked their whips, and made clear they wanted to stop.

"Sit! Sit!" the white bearded dwarf urged.

The Legionnaires quickly sat. It was nice to have a break.

The dust in front of them slowly parted. They all saw that it was the 47th, marching away. The dwarves began to load the scorpions.

Chapter 28

It all happened so quickly. The dwarves in their chairs at the back of the wagons quickly winched the scorpions back and put a bolt in the channel all by themselves. In just a few moments all ten scorpions were loaded and aimed at the slowly retreating 47th Legion. Simultaneously the dust cloud beside them suddenly became a mass of Ozani riders with bows, trotting to a good shooting range and wisely staying clear of the scorpions.

"NO!" a single Legionnaire in front of one of the scorpion wagons rose to his feet. He turned and threw himself at the wagon, trying to climb on top, to get at the dwarf, to stop the machine from firing.

The dwarf coolly drew a small crossbow and shot the man in the head. The blood flew backwards into the air, time seemingly slowing as all watched the man fall and then hit the ground.

The Legionnaires rose as one. Titus jumped to his feet too because it was like they were all connected by invisible rope, each pulling the other up. Some were shouting words, others screaming incoherently, like Titus. They threw themselves at the wagons. The dwarves did not even appear to be surprised. Each had a pair of small crossbows which they fired at the charging Legionnaires. The man standing beside Titus was hit in the shoulder and the power of the shot spun him around and pushed him to the ground. Even if all the dwarves had been skilled enough to take down two Legionnaires that still left two or more coming at them. Titus and another Legionnaire climbed up on a wagon and tried to get to the back. The dwarf was screaming at them, eyes wide and wild with hate. The Legionnaire grabbed a scorpion bolt as he advanced and held it like a knife. Titus bent to grab a bolt from the pile in the wagon but when his hands closed on it he lost his footing and fell out of the wagon. His anger was such that he tumbled on the ground and kept going, still holding the bolt. The dwarf focused its full attention on the other Legionnaire. From it's scorpion chair, the dwarf, now sword in hand, was swinging at the human as the Legionnaire stabbed back in return.

From being a stickman Titus knew that the bolts were sharp but not sharp enough to stab through armor by hand. Instead he swung it at the dwarf's ear, which wasn't covered by it's helmet. He swung with everything he had but the blow just seemed to startle the dwarf rather than hurt him. The creature turned its attention to Titus, who was right beside him. The other Legionnaire launched himself and pushed the dwarf out of the

I. Sylvano

scorpion seat on to the ground. Without thinking Titus was on top
of him, the bolt in his hand raised above the dwarf's face. He
drove it hard into the creature's eye. Even though the bolt went in
quite far the dwarf still struggled and thrashed. The other
Legionnaire was there too now, smacking his bolt into the dwarf's
face. The dwarf was flopping around like a fish pulled from the
sea. It finally let go of it's sword and the Legionnaire grabbed it
and plunged it into the thrashing dwarf's neck.

Titus looked around. Legionnaires were attacking the dwarves
with varying success. He saw that the white bearded dwarf had
killed all four Legionnaires and was now reloading his crossbows.
Titus climbed up into the scorpion seat. He was no marker but he
knew enough about scorpions to fake it. The dwarven scorpions
could turn like a turret and Titus adjusted the aim and fired. White
beard looked up just before the bolt hit him, surprise on his face
and then he was gone, in the air and tumbling, tumbling
backwards.

"Help me!" Titus screamed at the other Legionnaire.

The man still had the dwarf's sword in his hand. Titus was
trying to wind the scorpion by himself but the dwarven machinery
had been designed for the strength of dwarven arms. The other
Legionnaire understood at once and dropped the sword and helped
Titus ratchet for another shot. When Titus had locked it in place
and was putting another bolt in the channel the other Legionnaire
picked up the sword and ran to help his comrades fight the
dwarves.

The Legionnaires were swarming all over the dwarves and it
was hard for Titus to find a clear target. Then he saw the dwarf
leader. The vile creature had just thrown a Legionnaire off the
wagon and was standing tall and alone. Titus began working the
turning mechanism so that the scorpion pointed at the dwarf leader.
Blackbeard saw what Titus was doing and climbed back in his
scorpion seat and turned it towards Titus. The dwarf was much
faster than Titus and they both stopped at the same time, and then
fired. Titus pulled the pin and turned the motion into a fall that
had him off the wagon and on the ground. He heard the bolt
whoosh over his head, barely missing. When he poked his head
back up Blackbeard was gone. He looked behind him and saw that
the dwarf's bolt had travelled far and crashed through the Ozani

archers, who were now firing at the 47th.

Titus threw himself back into the scorpion seat and tried to ratchet the rope back. He tried with all his strength, cursing and praying but he wasn't strong enough. Then another hand grabbed on and together Titus and Tenax cranked it back. Titus put a bolt in the channel. Most of the Legionnaires and dwarves were dead. There were about twenty humans left, and ten or so dwarves running away.

"Shoot them!" Tenax screamed.

Titus turned the scorpion to face the Ozani riders. He fired and watched the bolt hit the mass of horse archers, splashing men and mounts all around it. Tenax ran to another scorpion, while shouting at a Legionnaire to help Titus. They loaded and shot into the Ozani again. The horse archers had stopped firing at the Romans and were beginning to panic. They loaded the two scorpions again and other Legionnaires watched and tried to do the same. They fired again. One of the Legionnaire aimed weapons managed to fire but the bolt shot into the ground with an explosion of grass and dirt. Another scorpion had not been correctly released and the man's arm had been caught. The rope pulled him forward and smashed him into the two columns at the front, killing him.

A few arrows were beginning to fall around the scorpion wagons. The Legionnaire who was helping Titus wind the ratchet jerked and hollered and as an arrow hit him in the shoulder. He didn't stop though. Titus and Tenax shot again, and this time the Ozani began to move, flowing like a flock of birds, over the hill and away. The other Legionnaire managed a good high shot but the horseman had already moved and the bolt sailed through the air and out of sight.

They began to cheer, shaking their fists in the air. The 47th was too far away to see what had happened- the dwarven equipment had an extra long range.

"Who's got legs?" A Legionnaire called out.

"I do!" Titus shouted. His had been a head injury and he could run.

He jumped off the wagon and ran towards the 47th. He ran out of breath half way there and had to slow but he forced himself onward, almost falling, gasping and shouting *Vigilanti! Vigilanti! Vigilanti!*

Chapter 29

The 47th had paused. They'd been retreating under fire for days. The Ozani archers had ridden off, leaving the skies clear for a little while. Senior Tribune Politio had called a halt. The 1st cohort had been on rearguard duty, under the command of First Spear Castus. The crusty older centurion hadn't needed one moment to think about the situation; he sent a runner to Politio and ordered half the 1st cohort to the dwarven scorpions battery.

Titus had led the way back and even though he was exhausted he was grinning from ear to ear. First Spear Castus had taken approximately three seconds to look at the dwarven wagon scorpions before giving the order to capture them and pull them to back to the 47th. Titus and the newly freed Legionnaires didn't even have to pull the wagons. They just had to keep up, which was hard enough for Titus, having already made the trip twice before.

The 47th had waited. Most of the Legionnaires were on the ground, exhausted. Most were forcing themselves to eat and drink. A few were taking the pause to empty their bowels. Even though the Ozani and the dwarfs had been constantly attacking them, there were at least two thirds left, which sounds positive until you consider that one third was dead or left to die.

Senior Tribune Politio was waiting, seated on the ground as the 1st cohort arrived with the captured artillery wagons. A Legionnaire beside him helped him to his feet, for the older man had knee problems.

"Well now," the tribune said, his eyes twinkling as he surveyed the wagon scorpions, "this might change things a little." His smile suggested that he was making an understatement.

Optio Sedo was summoned but couldn't be found. Three dozen Libritors arrived instead. The tired markers and stickmen oohed and ahhed the captured weapons.

Castus looked a little drunk, he was so happy. "We can use Legionnaires to pull them," he said. "That's what those poor blokes were being forced to do." He indicated the small group of wilted former prisoners. "Until they turned on the mercenaries."

his smiled deserted him. "Benzat," he said.

Politio mirrored his dark expression. "They'll not take this lightly." Politio looked up at the sky, judging the amount of daylight left. "Bring an inventory of the amount of ammunition," he said. "We've got three more hours of marching before we break."

"Yes, sir!" Castus said with a salute.

It seemed a little cruel to Titus that they'd fought their captors, defeated them, escaped, rejoined the Legion and were now being forced to march again. His legs did what they were told even as the rest of him complained. Titus wasn't sure if they marched for three more hours. The marching seemed unending yet when they halted his was shocked because the time had whizzed by like a close call scorpion bolt.

Politio had chosen some higher ground and the Legionnaires dug a deep ditch and used the dirt and turf to make a wall above. The wagon scorpions were placed around the barrier at intervals, staffed by pairs of Libritors. The First Spear had suggested the men who'd been prisoners be excused from duties and allowed to rest but Titus volunteered to go back to the wagon scorpions.

Most of the men were deep asleep, even though the sun had just set. Apparently they'd been marching at night too, under the constant storm of Ozani arrows. The horse archer tribesmen hadn't been seen since the Legion had recovered the wagon scorpions.

Titus stepped carefully. He'd been assigned to the East wall. After being lost in the grassland it was nice to have directions again. Legionnaires lied on the ground in large groups, snoring. There were no fires or torches- nothing that would give the enemy targets. Once Titus had finally arrived at the East side he found the Libritors waiting quietly beside the scorpions. He didn't know if specific ones had been assigned, so he found his way to one which only had one artillery man beside it.

"Can I join you?" Titus called out at the man, who seemed to be just a dark shadow at the other end of the wagon.

Titus could see the man turn, and then suddenly he began running at Titus. His head told him to raise his fists and draw his dagger but his body was too slow and tired and the man collided with him and knocked Titus to the ground.

"I can't believe it's you!" Glaber said. "I was sure you were dead!"

Titus laughed until a Legionnaire on watch told him to keep it quiet. The whole camp was under orders to be as silent as possible so that they might better hear any one sneaking up on them.

"They say they're going to come," Glaber whispered.

Titus was tired and his brain felt scrambled. He still had a painful lump on his forehead. "No idea what you're talking about," he whispered back.

"The Benzat," Glaber said.

Titus shook his head.

"The mercenary dwarves. They're Benzat. It's a tribe. They're- well they don't behave like humans. This is their equipment. They'll be back for it."

Titus shrugged, though he knew that Glaber couldn't see the movement in the darkness.

"They like to attack at night," Glaber said.

"Quiet!" hissed a passing Legionnaire.

Titus tried to stay awake. The thought of the black bearded dwarves creeping back through the darkness was actually rather terrifying, but Titus had been through too much. He fell asleep underneath the wagon, his soft snores joining in with the rest of the sleeping chorus.

A horn awakened him. It made him smile. The horns were Roman, they meant time to get up, they meant safety and purpose.

The sun was up and Glaber was awake, standing in the wagon. Titus climbed up to look too. In the distance, a large mass of Ozani horsemen were approaching, kicking up the dust.

They cranked back the scorpion as other scorpion wagons from the other walls were wheeled over. Titus fit a bolt into the channel. The Ozani seemed to be holding position.

"Do not fire!" First Spear Castus called, walking along the East wall. "We do not have a lot of ammunition. Do not fire unless I say!"

The Ozani came no closer and the order was never given. Eventually they took the bolts out of the channels and released the rope.

Legionnaires began pushing the walls down while others packed up. Glaber and Titus sat on their wagon and had a stale bread breakfast as the dust rose around them. Titus asked a

Legionnaire who said that no, there'd been no sign of the dwarves.

Chapter 30

Although a distant dust cloud followed the 47th, their spirits were much improved. The Ozani didn't wish to face the scorpions, and that was fine with the Legion. They marched at a normal pace, without incident. One more day and they'd be back to the road. Already the landscape was changing and there were pockets of trees and outcrops of rocks. Each step moved them further away from the grasslands and the horse archers.

Today the rear guard was the 4th cohort, along with half the scorpion wagons. Two Libritors had been assigned to each artillery piece, along with four Legionnaires to pull it. Titus and Glaber worked on the same scorpion. They'd taken to calling themselves XII section. They'd both gone to see Tenax several times in the hospital group. He recognized them but he seemed a change man. Like someone had opened him up and scraped him out- leaving him empty.

Titus had actually begun to enjoy the last day. The pace was reasonable and they were pushing on the back of the wagon. Spirits were high. All of the Legionnaires on the wagon were singing as they pulled and the sound was raucous and joyful. They were heading back to Dertona and Titus was excited to visit his brothers and see how they were doing. He did his best not to think about Elonia. Titus would stay away from the town and not go anywhere near her home. He never wanted to see her again.

That's what he was thinking when the ground in front of him erupted. Actually erupted, and something came out, something dressed in black with a black beard and an axe. All around the Benzat dwarves pushed out of their hiding spots in the dirt and began hacking at the scorpions. When the Legionnaires tried to stop them they attacked the Legionnaires. Then the arrows came.

"Form line form line!" a centurion named Carmenius was shouting.

The Legionnaires formed a solid shield wall against the direction the Ozani were firing from. Horns were sounded from the rest of the Legion. Titus had his sword out and was watching as the Benzat dwarf hacked through two Legionnaires as the Ozani arrows fell. One struck the dwarf in the arm. The dwarf ignored it. Titus couldn't just stand there, even though he had no confidence or skill with a sword. He came up behind the dwarf and slashed down at his head. Titus' gladius rang as the sword hit the metal helmet and bounced off. The dwarf turned suddenly, sweeping the axe at Titus. He tried to scramble back but his feet seemed to get tangled and he fell on to the ground on his back just before the axe passed over him. The dwarf probably looked down at him but Titus could only see the black beard. The dwarf raised his axe above his head, preparing to kill Titus. A pilum struck the dwarf in the chest, penetrating armour. Then a second pilum hit, followed by a third. Titus rolled to the side as quickly as he could and got to his feet. The dwarf was staring at him. Then the creature looked at the pila in its chest, and its knees collapsed. After a moment it fell forward. For a moment the pila held it off the ground, but then they gave way and the dwarf fell to the dirt.

"Get those scorpions firing!" First Spear Castus shouted. He pointed at Titus. "Get the scorpions firing!"

All of the Benzat dwarves were dead. They'd damaged or destroyed five of the scorpions, including Section XII's. Castus rushed at Titus and the young Libritor thought for a moment that the First Spear was going to attack him. At the last moment he raised his shield over Titus' head. An instant later the arrows struck; two thwacking loudly into the shield. Titus looked up and saw a pair of sharp metal points poking through.

Castus lowered his shield and shouted in Titus' face. "Fire the scorpions!"

Quickly they turned the surviving machines around and began to fire. The Ozani retreated immediately. They didn't disappear entirely, they stopped just out of range of the scorpions.

Titus helped load the wounded on to the wagons. They left the dead dwarves where they lay. Their attack had baffled Titus. What had they hoped to accomplish? Twenty or so dwarves against a Legion?

They marched for the rest of the day, not stopping until dusk. The Legionnaires built a marching camp. It was the same setup as the night before- a ditch with a turf wall and all the scorpions arranged along the perimeter

Glaber and Titus had been assigned to a new scorpion wagon. Twelve Libritors had died during the day- most had been killed by the dwarves, the rest by arrows.

Titus and his friend were lying under the wagon. Not asleep. They were supposed to be on standby in case of an attack.

"It doesn't make sense to me either," Glaber said. "It was a suicide mission."

"Someone was saying it was about honor," Titus said.

Glaber shook his head. "What's honourable about dying? So they killed a few men and broke a few machines. Did it make a difference? I don't think it did."

Titus thought about the difference one death could make. He was thinking of course of his father. He and his brothers were free of a bully, but their father had also stood up for them and raised them. He wondered where the honor was in his family situation. He'd already decided that he was going to visit his young brothers and give them as much of his pay as he could. That's where the honour was.

"What are you going to do when we get to Dertona?" Titus asked. "I heard we're all going to get leave."

"I don't have anywhere to go," Glaber said.

"You said you grew up on a farm," Titus said.

Glaber shook his head. "It's changed. I don't want to talk about it."

"Want to come to my family's farm?" Titus asked.

Glaber didn't say anything, so Titus didn't either. Above the two moons shone down with a river of stars between them.

"I talked to a Legionnaire today who said he saw Sedo die," Glaber said.

"How?"

"Arrows. Two of them. Before you returned and we got the scorpion wagons." Glaber banged on the bottom of the wagon with his boot. "One in his back and one in his thigh. He kept falling. Couldn't keep up," Glaber said.

Titus knew what that meant. The Legionnaires had killed him. A mercy murder. Better to die quick and clean on a Legion sword than be tortured by enemies. Titus imagined it happening to him. Arrows in his legs, or maybe he'd fallen off the wagon and broken his ankle. Well they had the wagons now and were putting the wounded in with the scorpions. Titus wondered if Glaber would kill him. Probably. Titus didn't think he could kill another Legionnaire. Especially a friend.

Chapter 31

It looked like the whole town had turned out to welcome the Legion back to Dertona. Probably the 47th had sent scouts ahead. Titus had heard stories of triumphant marches- citizens throwing flowers, women waving, offering wine- at this moment he was proud to be a member of the Legion.

At first there had been cheers, but they had quickly faded as they crowd took in the condition of the Legionnaires. They were dirty and bloody. There was no baggage train. Titus could hear people crying. They'd left one third of their number dead in the grass. People were calling out to the Legionnaires and they were calling back. The usual prim and proper march enforced by the centurions was nowhere to be seen. How many centurions hadn't made it home?

Titus saw women and families collapse as the news was called out to them by passing Legionnaires, as if the people were suddenly melting or their leg bones had turned to jelly. The small force of Legionnaires that had stayed behind at the base had formed up as an honour guard, lining both sides of the street in front of the base as the 47th marched through the gates. They continued in to the camp parade ground where they halted and waited for the honour guard. The centurion in charge saluted and turned over command to the First Spear and Senior Tribune.

Politio climbed stiffly onto the small platform- he'd walked the entire way, just like everybody else- he took his time looking over the assembled troops. Now all was truly silent. Except birds were singing. It made Titus smile. They'd made it back. They were the lucky ones.

"Comrades!" Politio called out loudly. "Legionnaires of the 47th *Vigilanti!*"

The Legion roared back at him.

"We have come through the brown grass!" Politio shouted. "And lived to tell the tale!"

Again the Legionnaires roared.

"Gather your strength. Rest your wounds. Because it three weeks we go back for our vengeance!"

Again the roar, a little more muted. *Three weeks.* In three weeks they'd go back to finish the job they'd failed at. Subduing the Ozani threat.

They were dismissed. For a moment they all stood there, conscious of the fact that as soon as they took a step away they were leaving something that would disappear- a brotherhood forged of their recent struggle. It was only for a few moments, and then they broke away, to their barracks, to make their reports- no longer a single organism but instead individual men.

There seemed to be no one in charge of the sad bedraggled Libritors. They'd been left in charge of the scorpion wagons by default and eventually had begun pulling them to the artillery headquarters. Though it wasn't difficult work Titus realized that he was very tired.

Half of the Libritors had not made it back. Titus and Glaber retired to section XII's barrack. It didn't really feel like home because they'd spent almost no time there. Eventually Tenax limped in. He truly looked awful. He'd lost a noticeable amount of weight and his face seemed pale in comparison to his dark hair. All the fire in him- the anger- was missing. He plunked down onto his bed and lay down without saying a word.

The horns awoke all the next morning. Titus would have slept later.

"I guess we report to Artillery," Glaber said.

Tenax was just sitting up as the two younger men went out the door. It felt good to be wearing only their tunics. It was cooler here than it was in the grassland, and there were white puffs of cloud in the sky.

The Libritors were still arriving when a man with an optio's two- feathered helmet called for attention. Every one stopped and stood straight.

"Relax," the man said with a smile. "You're Libritors, not Legionnaires. I'm your new adjutant officer, Optio Ayus Nipius Lagois."

"Welcome," Mergo from section VIII called out.

"As you heard yesterday we're going back into the field in three weeks or so. We have three things to accomplish before then." He held a finger up. "We need to repair the broken dwarven scorpions. I have every confidence that we can do that. We need to recruit more Libritors- you can leave that to me. And we've been ordered to mount our own Roman scorpions on to wagons."

"The dwarven ones can swivel," someone said. "Are we going to get that kind of gear in three weeks?"

"I don't know," Optio Lagois admitted. "Second thing." He held up two fingers. "Pay parade."

The Libritors cheered.

"The Senior Tribune has ordered that everyone be paid before lunch."

More cheering. Could anything be better than pay and then lunch?

He held up a third finger. "Leave. The Senior Tribune has decreed that every man shall receive three days leave over the next three weeks. You will come to me to schedule it. Those with the most seniority will be going first."

"Which makes us last," Titus whispered to Glaber.

Glaber shrugged.

"Split into your sections, gather your equipment and find out what needs to be done. The smiths and tinkers will be here this afternoon. Questions?"

"Where do I sign up for leave?" Mergo shouted.

Everyone began talking. Eventually they formed up into their twelve sections. Few had all four members and there were several with only one member. Two sections were empty. Tenax arrived, limping, just before pay parade.

It was decided that section XII would receive one of the dwarven scorpion wagons and one of the normal Roman ones that supposedly was to be put on a wagon as well. Were they going to be pulled by mules, Titus wondered? The entire Legion was going to be looking for mules. Surely there weren't that many in Dertona.

Tenax sat on the ground and watched as Glaber and Titus examined section XII's dwarven scorpion wagon. It was one of the broken ones. You could easily see where the gears that made the scorpion swivel had been smashed. One of the scorpion arms had been struck too, and cracked. Although it was still in one piece it wouldn't be safe to use.

Optio Lagois conducted the pay parade in the yard behind Artillery headquarters. The clerks from finance had their ledgers. Glaber, Titus and Tenax were paid 100 denarii; a little less than some of the others because the three were new recruits who'd already received an advance. Still, it was a lot of money and Titus was looking forward to giving it to his brothers when he visited them on leave.

Chapter 32

In the afternoon the metal workers and craftsmen from the town came to view the dwarven equipment. The 47th's chief engineer, Pietus Mollus Arenea toured them through the functioning wagon scorpions and then onto the ones in need of repair. Titus was supposed to be doing an inventory of bolts, but he listened in, fascinated as they examined section XII's mangled scorpion.

"We can repair that arm, no problem," a man said. He was short and wide with thick meaty arms. If he'd had a beard he would've looked like a tall dwarf. "This is another matter."

Titus peeked to see what the man was talking about. The speaker was pointing at the gear construction that made the scorpion swivel on the wagon.

"That's not steel- that's steel mixed with somewhat else," the man continued. "you can see that it's under a lot of strain but it takes it no problem."

"Can you copy it?" Engineer Arenea asked.

The man let out a loud mouthful of air. "In three weeks? No. Definitely no. Maybe in a year."

Can you change the base of the scorpions we usually make so that we can mount them on a wagon?" Arenea asked.

"That we can do," the man said. "If you can find enough wagons."

That was to be the story of the next two weeks. There were not enough mules. There were not enough wagons. There were not enough scorpion bolts.

Titus, Glaber and Tenax watched as the repairs proceeded on the broken dwarven machine. The damaged arm was removed and replaced with a similar one, made of thin layers of wood and steel glued together. The busted gear configuration that had enabled the scorpion to swivel was removed and the scorpion bolted to the wagon, unmoveable, facing forward. The Legion's metalworkers and smiths began to produce steel bolts that would fit both the dwarven equipment and the usual human version.

A new bunch of recruits also arrived. A balding, pot-bellied fellow in his thirties named Capio became the fourth member of Section XII. Although Tenax was recovering physically he still seemed empty of that fire that had burned in him- which turned out to be a blessing because Capio talked too much. He had an annoying mule-like laugh and he brayed at all his own jokes. Tenax didn't look happy, but he tolerated the new man. They were also issued with a regular Roman scorpion that had been bolted to the back of a wagon. Titus and Glaber took the new human designed one and Tenax and Capio practised with the dwarven machine.

Finally, the day came for Titus to take his three-day leave. Glaber had said he wasn't going to take any but Titus convinced him to tag along and visit Titus' brothers.

"You'll have fun!" Titus encouraged.

"No I won't,' Glaber said. "But I'd had enough of this base and the 47th and a little break will be nice."

Titus walked out the front gate with his full 100 denarii. Glaber had given half of his to the Libritor's burial fund but he was interested in spending the rest. Against Titus' wishes they stopped at the market and Glaber bought some wine. Titus purchased a bag of apples to give to his brothers.

Titus poked Glaber in the forearm. "That's her," he said, motioning with his head.

"Who?"

"The woman...the one that took all of the money," Titus said. "Elonia."

She was chatting and flirting, turning her head this way and that so that her long dark hair shone. If she noticed Titus she was ignoring him. Behind her, ten paces away, her husband Marco was watching. He stared hard at Titus and then bared his teeth like an animal.

"Let's go," Titus said.

Glaber shrugged and they left. Titus wondered if Marco had been watching from somewhere all the times he'd been with Elonia. He wondered how many other men had fallen for their little game.

He began to feel better as they left the town behind. His family's farm was about an hour walk from Dertona.

He knew that Glaber didn't want to talk about his family, but they'd opened the wine and had been sharing it and his tongue got away from him. "Is your family from Dertona?"

Glaber's smile disappeared and he was suddenly serious. "I said I didn't want to talk about them. I'll turn around and march right back to the base."

"Sorry."

Titus found it strange being near his home again. There were lots of memories, all conflicting. It was lovely to see the trees and fields he knew so well. Yet there was the old oak he'd hidden behind for an entire day when his father was in a rage. He smiled when he saw the house in the distance. As they drew nearer he was happy to see that it was in good condition. Haven't been gone that long really, he reminded himself.

There was no one home when they arrived. Titus gave Glaber a quick tour. In previous days Titus' father had occupied one bedroom and all three boys the other. From the look of things, they'd each taken one now. The floor was spotless, the dishes clean and there was food in the larder. Titus knew it was because of Appius, Titus' 14-year-old brother. He'd always been more focused and hard working than Titus. Tullus was only 9 and was more interested in exploring the nearby river than anything else.

Titus recognized his brother's voices as they approached the house. He went outside so he didn't scare them. They stopped when they saw him, and then came running as soon as they knew who it was. They had a long group hug and Tullus cried.

"What's it like?" Appius asked. "We heard stories that the Legion was fighting."

Titus nodded. "I'll tell you later. First, I want you to meet my friend."

He introduced Glaber, who made a gift of the already opened jug of wine. Appius made supper while Tullus helped Titus make a place for the two Libritors to sleep.

"We can sleep in here," Titus said, indicating the common room. "Believe me, we've slept in worse. I don't want to turf you out of your rooms."

Appius talked about how things were going on the farm. He sounded disinterested, but he obviously knew what he was doing. Their father had made them do pretty much everything and so it hadn't matter so much when he'd died.

"Appius has a girl friend!" Tullus gleefully informed.

He didn't deny it. "Her name is Letitia," he said. "She lives on the farm on the other side of the river."

"She's nice," Tullus admitted. "They kiss."

They had a simple supper and then cleaned up. Appius and Titus went for a walk to look at the river- Titus wanted to see where Letitia lived. When they left Glaber was telling wild stories to Tullus and making him laugh.

"I'm sorry for everything that happened," Titus said to his brother.

Appius shrugged. It was his typical response. His eyes grew large though when Titus gave him all of his money.

"Put it somewhere safe and DON'T give it to a girl," Titus warned. "Promise me that."

Appius promised. "See, there." He was pointing at a little farm house in the distance across the river. "That's where she lives."

"Just be careful," Titus said, though he knew Appius always was.

"How long have you and Glaber been together?" Appius asked.

"We're in the same section," Titus answered, then realized what his brother was really asking. "We're not together."

"Oh. I thought maybe she was your girlfriend."

"What are you talking about? Glaber's in the Legion. He's a man. He's just thin, like me, and doesn't have much facial hair." Titus trailed off, realization slowly dawning.

"I think it's obvious he's a girl," Appius said. "He's got girl legs."

Chapter 33

Titus and Appius were sitting on the river bank. They'd stripped off their sandals and had their feet in the cool water. It was more of a stream at this point; clear cold water rippling and racing over the rocks. It was only knee deep in the centre.

"I've been looking at girls," Appius said. When he focused on something he was very thorough. "They have different hands, necks- well, pretty much everything."

"Glaber said he grew up on a farm," Titus said. "I mean she." He still was finding it hard to believe. "His hands and arms are as big as mine."

Appius laughed. "Tullus' are as big as yours. You're a stick, Titus."

"Why would a girl join the Legion?" Titus asked.

"Why did you?"

"To escape."

Appius began kicking his feet in the water, splashing. "Maybe I'm wrong. But he's not very hairy."

"Neither am I."

"Actually if you look closely, you are, it's just all blonde." Appius continued to splash with his feet.

Titus looked up, someone on the other side of the river was coming towards them. A girl. A young woman. She was skipping happily. Titus understood then. This was their meeting place- Appius and his girl. The splashing was probably their signal.

"How old is she?" Titus whispered to his brother.

"Fifteen."

She came to the rivers edge and kicked off her sandals. She dipped her toes into the cool stream and then tried to playfully kick water at the two brothers.

"This is Letitia," Appius introduced. "This is my older brother, Titus."

Laetitia was cute. She had brown hair and her skin was tanned by the sun. She smiled a cheery gap toothed smile. Titus noticed that her arms were bigger than his- and they weren't fat arms. They were muscled farm worker arms.

"Nice to meet you," Titus said.

She grinned. "I'm glad you didn't die in the war."

"Me too." Titus had begun to feel like he was intruding. He pulled his cold toes out of the stream and put his sandals back on. "I'm going to go back the house," he announced. "It was nice meeting you."

The love birds didn't acknowledge his departure. They were already staring and chirping at each other.

Could it be true? Could Glaber be a girl? A woman? In a way, he felt like it was something he'd always known. He really liked Glaber. He'd consider him- her- his best friend. Glaber was easy to be around. It had been different with Elonia. But that wasn't real, he reminded himself. Elonia was always posing and trying to be cute. Playing at being a bubbly girl. What if a woman didn't do that? Would they be just like a man?

Titus slowed his pace as he drew near the house. He didn't know what he was going to say. Maybe he should just keep his mouth shut. Maybe Appius was wrong. There were thin hairless men.

Light laughter floated on the evening air. Tullus and Glaber were joking. Tullus' guffaw sounded like a young boy's. Glaber's laughter seemed to be on the line- maybe female, maybe male.

"What are you guys laughing at?" Titus said, stepping through the door.

"Telling Legion stories," Glaber said with a smile. "Remember the time Allec got stuck in the latrine?"

Titus nodded. "Isn't it your bedtime Tullus?"

His little brother looked shocked. Likely he hadn't thought of such a thing after their father had died.

"I go to bed when Appius does," Tullus said sulkily. "he doesn't get home until after dark."

Appius' romance must be quite serious, Titus thought. "Glaber do you want to go for a walk around the farm?"

"Sure."

"Can I come?" Tullus asked.

"Not this time," Titus said.

Glaber gave him a strange look.

The two Libritors went outside. It was almost sundown now. Already both moons were peeking above the horizon.

"How big is the farm?" Glaber asked.

Titus led his friend away from the house. He'd tried to convince himself that he wasn't going to ask. That it didn't matter. But he was doing it anyway. It reminded him of the times he'd been with Elonia. It hadn't felt right, but he hadn't wanted to stop.

"Titus?"

"Sorry, I was thinking." There was a nervous quiver in Titus' stomach. "It's strange, being back."

"How big is the farm?" Glaber asked again.

"Not big," Titus said. "As far as the river that way, and there's other small farms on other side. Enough to live on, not get rich."

"Can we go to the river?"

"No, please, tomorrow? Appius is meeting his girl out there. I think they do it every night."

Glaber said nothing.

Titus walked his friend to the one edge of his family's land. "This is as far as it goes this way. See the line of stones?" In the growing darkness Titus couldn't see what expression Glaber had. "What was your family farm like?"

"I don't want to talk about it."

"Glaber?"

"What?"

He couldn't do it. Titus couldn't say the words. He wasn't sure why. Because he didn't want to know. Because he didn't want things to change. Glaber was the best friend he'd ever had.

"What Titus?" Glaber asked.

"Oh, nothing." He looked up at the sky. Both moons had a greenish tinge. "Do you know what it means when the moons look like that?"

"Something about not eating fish because it spoils faster," Glaber said. "My family didn't believe in moon lore."

"I'm glad you came to meet my brothers," Titus said.

Glaber put a friendly hand on Titus' shoulder. "Thanks for inviting me. Let's go back and tease Tullus' some more."

"And have some of that wine," Titus added. He'd decided to believe that Appius was wrong. Glaber was a young man, just like himself.

Chapter 34

Three days' leave passed like an afternoon. It felt strange to be away from the Legion, where you were always either working or recovering. Titus and Glaber helped out on the farm, chiefly working on a new rock fence. Titus was surprised that he didn't get tired as quickly as he used to. Maybe he had gotten stronger.

Tullus hugged both Titus and Glaber when it was time for them to leave. Appius of course was serious and formal, shaking each of their hands.

"Thank you," Glaber said, as they walked back to town. "I had my doubts but I was wrong. I had a nice time."

Titus just nodded. He didn't know what to say. He knew Glaber wouldn't talk about his own family or past. Although he was pretending that he was confident that Glaber was male there was still a little part of him that wasn't sure.

"You're not very talkative," Glaber said.

"Just thinking about my father," Titus lied. But it was a raw enough subject that Glaber became quiet too.

Dertona was busy and you could feel the energy. The Legion was going to be leaving in a day or two and a lot was happening- merchants selling supplies, metalworkers and craftsmen doing repairs, wives and girlfriends saying goodbye, prostitutes doing brisk business. Titus purposely looked the other way when a middle-aged woman called out to them as they passed- he felt like he didn't know what to say around Glaber anymore. Glaber just waved at the woman as they continued.

The camp smelled of fresh baked bread and animal shit. When they arrived at artillery HQ Titus heard that there hadn't been enough mules available, even though it didn't smell that way.

"They've assigned Legionnaires to pull the scorpion wagons," Optio Lagois explained to the group of Libritors. "At least we'll be safer if we get overrun," he said with a laugh.

No one else found it funny. The new recruits were just scared and the more experienced were remembering the Ozani arrows and heavy cavalry.

The next two days were extremely busy. Section XII now had two wagon scorpions, though neither could swivel. If you needed to shoot in a different direction you had to move the wagon. New leather covers had been made to put over the weapons to protect the ropes and mechanisms from the weather. Titus, Glaber, Tenax and the new guy Capio packed Section XII's wagons with supplies of bolts, a tarp, a tent, food, water and their weapons and shields. They left room for the Legionnaires' kit too, since the soldiers would be pulling the wagon and not carrying the gear.

The night before they left they were given free time to do as they pleased. Section XII, like many in the Legion, spent the evening drinking wine.

Capio had purchased several jugs and they were sitting in their barracks room passing the first one around. Capio seemed anxious to be friendly and Titus suspect that the new recruit also really liked wine, judging from his pot belly.

"I used to work in the iron mines," Capio said, "but that was too grim. Half of the workers are slaves or convicts. Then I tried working in construction, building houses. The unrest caused by the Ozani ruined that. People are moving away, not building new places." Capio liked to talk. "I have a few debts," he laughed. "Nothing too serious. That's why I joined up. How about you?"

"I don't have the skills for anything else," Tenax said. "I was a private guard before this. Broke my leg in an accident. The Legion thought I'd make a good Libritor."

"I needed a job," Titus said. "And wanted to get away from my father."

No one said a word about what had happened to Titus' Dad.

"What about you Glaber?" Capio said. "Why are you here?"

"Wanted to see the world," Glaber said.

Capio laughed and laughed. Somehow, he seemed to have gotten really drunk while the rest of them were still warming. He motioned at the walls of the barracks. "Nice view! What do you think of the world so far?"

Glaber, Tenax and Titus all turned in early. Capio couldn't seem to stay quiet so he went out to look for someone to talk to.

The horns sounded extra early the next morning. Leaving day. Titus and Glaber both got up right away, Tenax a moment after them. Capio was badly hung over. His face looked grey and he was groaning. They left him on his own and went to get breakfast.

"He'd better clean up his own puke," Tenax growled as they waited in line for some hot porridge with fruit.

When they arrived back at the barrack after eating Capio was lying on the floor beside a large puddle of vomit. Glaber grabbed his kit and immediately left. Tenax and Titus brought their chain mail and other gear outside. Tenax looked angrily.

"What do you want to do?" Titus said. "I can clean it up, I don't mind." It was true. He'd been the official cleaner of accidental bodily spills while growing up. Not because he liked it but because he was the oldest and his father made him.

Tenax frowned. "It's not fair," he said. "If we leave him he'll get in trouble. It's what he deserves. But we look out for each other too."

It was true. You relied on your comrades for everything. Capio had screwed up, but he was new. In the end Tenax and Titus decided to help. If they hadn't been marching out that morning they would have left him.

Tenax made Capio drink water, dress and pack and Titus cleaned the puke up. It still smelled like wine. They walked Capio to Artillery HQ, one on each side of him because he wasn't very steady.

Legionnaires from the 4th cohort were going to pull and they had already stowed their gear on the wagons. Niallus, the Libritor signifier was carrying their pennant, now decorated with one silver phalera with an eye painted on it. *Vigilanti.*

The horns sounded and the marching began. This time the Libritors were leading the way, in case the Ozani showed up. It wasn't likely they mounted tribesmen would be this far South but it was good practice.

The Ala went first, riding ahead to scout. The Libritors and the scorpion wagons clattered through the streets of Dertona, Legionnaires easily pulling them.

Titus wasn't sure how he felt. He'd been to war once already, and lived to tell the tale. Truthfully, he was a little excited. Staying on the base was boring. Glaber and Tenax seemed in good spirits too. Capio threw up by the side of the road and ended up riding in one of the wagons. The Legionnaires pulling promised to wait until he was feeling better before beating him up.

Chapter 35

They marched for five days without seeing anything beside the grass and sky. It was like the Ozani had vanished. There was lots of news. There were three other Legions in the grassland. They were all working together, trying to trap the horsemen. The 12th Legion *Victrix*, was to the North, the 22nd Legion *Magnum* coming from the West, and the vicious 26th Legion *Minotauro* was camped out in the grass to the East. The 47th was coming up from the South. Somewhere in the huge square of grassland between them, were the tribesmen.

The 47th's Ala were scouting and were constantly arriving and departing. Titus had no idea what they were reporting and the rumours covered absolutely everything: The Ozani had vanished; they'd joined with the Changsammi, another similar tribe; they were battling one of the other Legions and numerous other untruths. Titus tried not to listen or get worked up by the rumours. He tried to focus on the wagon scorpion- keeping it moving. That was all. Unless they were cresting a hill he couldn't see past the Legionnaires in the advance party and there was no point in looking anyway since there was nothing out there. There were no ambushes or night attacks. Just nothing. If Titus thought about fighting it was nerve-wracking. If he was able to focus on the wagon, chatting with Glaber and the Legionnaires or the bottomless blue sky it was almost peaceful. A family camping and picnic trip.

On the fifth day everything changed. The Ala scouts were coming and going more frequently, and they were riding harder. Rumours rippled through the ranks that the Ozani had been sighted ahead. Most importantly, there was a dust cloud in the sky. It was large enough that it either had to be the horsemen or another Legion.

A halt was called and Option Lagois rode by each section.

"This is it lads, be ready!" he called out with a smile.

"How close are they?" a Legionnaire asked.

Lagois laughed and pointed at the dust cloud in the sky. "Check your gear, have a bite, be ready. Watch the signfier." The Optio rode off to spread the word.

Titus helped Glaber take the cover off their wagon scorpion. Tenax and Capio did the same. The march resumed, with the Legionnaires pulling the wagon scorpions and the Libritors pushing from behind.

At first Titus was jumpy and nervous. As time wore on he began to relax. After two hours he wondered if they should put the cover back on. The scorpions could be fussy if their mechanisms and ropes were dusty or too hot. They were in a flatter area and there was nothing to see but the backs of the Legionnaires in front of them.

When there was a crashing sound and men screaming out Titus didn't understand what it was. It had been quiet- except for the grunts and chatter of the Legionnaires, the clink of their armour and the occasional buzz of a fly. At first Titus thought the crash was a scorpion wagon tipping over. Maybe there'd been a hole? Maybe some men had been injured. Moments later the second crash came. Titus and Glaber looked at each other, both realizing at the same instant- scorpions.

All at once everyone began shouting. No orders could be heard but everyone was doing the right things. The advance centuries of Legionnaires were going to ground and the scorpion wagons were being pulled forward. As Titus pushed on the back of his wagon a nearby one belonging to Section XI was hit. The incoming enemy bolt hit the scorpion itself, and it seemed to explode, pieces flying everywhere. Some of the flying pieces hit the men pulling and pushing. The weapon was completely ruined.

Optio Lagois came thundering by on his terrified horse. "Fire!" he screeched. "Fire!"

Glaber climbed up onto the wagon and got in the seat. Tenax did the same, a little slower because of his bad leg.

"There! There!" a Legionnaire was pointing and shouting.

In the distance, up on a little hill, were the enemy scorpions.

"Turn more to the right!" Glaber shouted, trying to get the Legionnaires at the front of the wagon to turn it so he could fire.

Titus was on the wagon too, fitting the bolt into the channel. He looked at Glaber. The young man looked scared.

"Clear!" Glaber shouted and the Legionnaires all dove to the ground.

Titus crouched by the wagon but Glaber didn't fire.

"Those are fucking dwarves again!" Glaber cursed. "They have longer range. I can't hit them."

There were ten captured dwarven scorpions and they began to fire. Titus looked over and saw Capio crouch by the wagon. Tenax fired and with a loud *whang!* the bolt disappeared. The enemy scorpions were so far away you couldn't really see if you hit anything. Tenax and Capio rewound the mechanism and Capio was fitting in another bolt when the scorpion's arm broke. It had been repaired in camp but the tension must have been to much. The breaking piece caught Capio as he was bent over the channel and threw him twenty feet. Tenax leaned out of the seat and slid onto the ground. A moment later an enemy bolt hit the scorpion and the entire wagon flipped.

Glaber, who was still in the marker seat shouted at the Legionnaires. "Get us out of here! Now!"

The Legionnaires, used to following orders, jumped to their feet and began pushing the wagon backwards. Most of the other human made scorpions were doing the same. The captured dwarven equipment was still firing but the enemy had good aim and was targeting and destroying them. They too started to retreat.

Titus ran forward to check on Capio. He was still lying in the grass, not moving. His eyes were open when Titus arrived. He looked up at Titus, a thin line of blood drooling out of the corner of his mouth.

"It hurts to move," he said. "It hurts. I'm hurt inside,"

There were several Medicuses already moving around, treating the injured. Titus waved at one and waited with Capio. The enemy soon stopped firing as the surviving Roman scorpion wagons were all pulling back. Titus waved at the Medicus again. He waved back- he'd be there as soon as he could. Titus felt the tremble in the earth just before he heard the hooves. He looked up. A large mass of Ozani horsemen were riding fast towards the Legion. Titus saw the wave of arrows leave their bows, looking like a swarm of insects lifting off into the sky.

The call went up among the Legionnaires and they crouched under their shields. The first wave of arrows hit, thwacking into the ground and pounding into the wooden shields and wagons. There were calls to set the scorpions up and fire at the Ozani. The horse archers released two more volleys of arrows. Titus and anyone else in front of the Legion were safe because the enemy was targeting the mass of soldiers and wagons further back. Titus saw men fall and cry out as arrows sneaked past their shields. Some writhed in the grass, like snakes whose tails are caught. Others fell silently and didn't move again. One Legionnaire somehow took an arrow in the eye; the arrow was almost straight up from his face and helmet. He was walking around like he was looking for something, blood running down his cheek. Then he stumbled, fell and laid still.

The scorpions were aimed and loaded but the Ozani had ridden off. There was nothing to shoot at.

The Medicus finally came to Titus and Capio. The Medicus was calm, even though his arms were covered in blood and there were red smears on his face. He gently probed Capio's ribs, causing the wounded man to cry out.

"There's nothing I can do. Get a stretcher and bring him to the field hospital," the Medicus said, and then ran off to look at a crying man whose face was covered with blood.

"Am I going to die?" Capio asked Titus.

Titus made himself smile. "Not today," he said. He had no idea if it was true.

Chapter 36

Making the camp brought back so many bad memories. The Legionnaires piled the turf squares into walls, leaving a knee deep ditch outside. The wagon scorpions were positioned along the walls. They didn't set up the tents, expecting a night attack of fire arrows. Instead they piled the shields ready to use. Titus and Glaber sat beside their wagon. They hadn't seen Tenax, who was fine, or Capio, who was not. Titus had waited with the new Libritor until three Legionnaires had come with a stretcher and together the four of them had carried Capio into the camp under construction.

"There's the other Legions," Glaber said, drawing Titus out of his dark thoughts.

"What about them?"

"The other Legions will push at the Ozani. Surround them. We won't be sitting here getting shot like last time."

Titus smiled a fake sickly smile. "Just tonight," he said.

Optio Lagois came around at sunset, checking on the equipment and the Libritors. He was also looking for volunteers.

"The Senior Tribune is sending a force out against the enemy scorpions," Lagois explained. "I've been asked it any Libritors are willing to go. If we capture them, we'll turn them on the Ozani."

"I'll go," said Titus.

Glaber looked at him, shocked. "They tried that last time if you remember," he said.

Titus remembered. A century had gone out and not returned.

"Politio is sending four centuries," the Option quickly said. "with a specific objective this time."

"I'll go," Titus said again. He wasn't being brave and he knew it. He was terrified. He didn't think he could face another night of sitting in the camp as arrows, fire and scorpion bolts rained down. Out in the grass you could at least run. Or hide.

Lagois nodded. "Good man. Report to center square." He walked on.

Glaber was still staring at him. Titus didn't know what to say.

"You'll get killed," Glaber said.

"If I see Tenax I'll send him over to be your stickman," Titus answered. He walked away angrily. What right did Glaber have to talk like that? It was Titus' choice. Glaber was acting like.... he shook the thought away. They were friends. That's all it was. Best friends. What would he say if Glaber had volunteered? He would have wished her well. Wished HIM well, he corrected himself. Glaber was a man. His friend.

There was much activity in the center square. Legionnaires were taking their armor off so they could move quietly in the grass. Titus remembered that he was supposed to look for Tenax. Oh well. He took his chain mail off. They'd dug a hole and put water and ash in it to make soupy mud. Titus joined the line to smear it on his face. A centurion walked by, reminding everyone that they were to bring two javelins each and leave their shields behind.

Titus didn't mind. He was a terrible shot with a pilum but he was also terrible with a shield. He really wouldn't be much use unless they captured the scorpions. An image of the fierce black bearded dwarves crossed his mind and he shuddered. He didn't really want to see more of them.

They crouched and sat in four circles as the centurions briefed everyone. They'd taken their helmets off, replaced them with normal Legionnaire helmets smeared with mud so they didn't reflect the moon light. Both moons were up; one was full and the other almost. A bright night.

"Libritors, welcome to the 5th century," the centurion said. "I'm Carmenius, and that sorry sod is the Optio, Titus. You're to stay with us."

There were eight Libritors. If they managed to overrun the scorpions the Legionnaires would handle the ratcheting and the Libritors would aim and fire. All the centuries going out were from the 4th cohort. 2nd century was bringing their shields, but they were keeping them in their canvas covers to make them darker. If the 3rd, 4th and 5th centuries found trouble they were to retreat to the shield wall of the 2nd century.

"Any questions?" Centurion Carmenius asked.

There were none.

As they started to move the barrage began on one side. Scorpion fire targeting the Roman machines behind the turf walls. Titus was relieved to see that it was on the opposite of Section XII's wagon.

"They'll try to wreck the scorpions so the horse archers can come in," someone said.

"Let's go!" Carmenius ordered. "MOVE! Do you want to stay around and wait for the arrows?"

Titus was glad to be leaving the camp. Quickly they trickled out the gate of the wall furthest from the side under attack. He saw Glaber and Tenax watching them. They didn't recognize him because his face was plastered with mud.

It was like being in a small herd of animals. Goats maybe. Silent goats, staying low, following the goat in front of you in the darkness. Keeping your pila points towards the ground. They began to run. Titus stole a glance back at the camp. The sky was full of light as fire arrows rained down on it.

They kept running. Titus had no idea where they were going. His job was to follow. They travelled around the side of a low hill and were told to go to ground. Titus collapsed into the grass, breathing hard like the Legionnaires around him. Or maybe they were Libritors. Everyone looked the same with their faces covered in mud.

Then they were up again, running, crouched. A large group of Legionnaires split off from the main group and went to the side, everyone running and staying low.

"Faster! Faster!" someone was hissing at them.

Again they went to ground. Grass all around them. Somehow Titus had banged his knee and it hurt. They lay quiet and still, mosquitos buzzing all around them. Then they were crawling. There was a taller hill ahead. On top of it were a group of horseman. Titus guessed maybe a hundred. They were like black cut-outs against the star speckled sky behind them.

"Get ready," the man beside Titus whispered. "Pass it on."

"Get ready," Titus said to the man on the other side. He turned back to the first on. "Ready for what?"

"Charging the hill."

Chapter 37

Titus was crouched at the bottom of the hill with a hundred or so others. They had no armor, no shields. Titus gripped a pilum in each hand. While he waited for the command to attack, he went over what he was going to do in his head. Stand, take two running steps, throw the pilum in his right hand. Make sure the pilum in his left hand was pointing down so he didn't injure his comrades. Pass the pilum from left to right hand. Take two running steps and throw. Draw gladius and run up the hill. You can do it, he kept telling himself. He'd never hit anything with a javelin before except the ground. While he was busy doubting himself the command came.

"Throw!"

Titus recognized Centurion Carmenius' voice in that brief instant. Then he was standing and taking two running steps while his head was still whirling and his eyes looking around. The horseman at the top of the hill still were dark shadows against the star sparkly sky. He threw. He tried not to watch but he wanted to watch. He was taking two more steps. The dark shadows at the top of hill burst into sudden chaotic motion as the javelins tore into them.

"Charge!" Carmenius' voice roared from somewhere.

The Legionnaires ran up the hill. Titus noticed that he still had the second javelin gripped tightly in his left hand. The dark shapes were starting to take on features; a horse staggering with three pila jammed into it; A screaming horseman waving a long curved sword; a man choking and crying, trying to pull a javelin out of his chest. Then the Legion hit. Titus still had the javelin so he gripped it with both hands instead of using his sword. A horse danced in front of him, its rider slashing frantically around him at the wary Legionnaires. But they only had their short swords. Titus stabbed forward into the horse's flank, putting his weight into it. The horse screamed and toppled to the side. The Legionnaires pounced and killed the rider. Another horseman rode by quickly and began striking at Titus with a blade. The sword hit Titus' helmet on an angle and skidded off. Titus was shocked, then angry. He turned to the horseman who was a dozen steps away by now and threw his pilum. The throw was all anger but it flew true and jammed into the rider at the base of his spine. The impact threw him off the terrified horse. Titus ran over, pulling his gladius as he went. The man was still alive, trying to roll over. Titus thrust his sword into the man's neck, saw his eyes bulge and look at Titus' moonlit face and then roll back into his head. Titus pulled the sword out, ready for the next combat.

Other Legionnaires had come in hard from the side. They were trying to kill all of the horsemen so they couldn't spread the word. Three horsemen were hacking at the Legionnaires, their horses kicking out with their legs. Titus ran to a downed dead mount and piled a pilum out. It was slightly bent, but he threw it anyway. The misshapen javelin flew off harmlessly to the side. What the hell had he done with his sword? He looked around frantically on the dark ground. He found a curved sword and ran screaming at the three riders who were fighting his comrades. His charge disrupted them, and he slashed at the back legs of two different horses. One of them kicked out at him and Titus struck with all his might and cut through the animal's thin leg. The horse went down, freaking with pain. The rider was trying to get free but Titus was behind him and started hacking at the man's neck and shoulders. Titus realized the man had armor so he switched to stabbing and pushed the blade into the man's back. The rider crumpled to the side, taking Titus' sword with him. He looked around for another weapon. A horse's ferocious frightened breathing warned him that another rider was upon him. His hands closed around something hard on the ground. He picked it up and threw it at the rider, only registering that it was a horse's severed leg as it left his hands. The oncoming rider ducked to the side to avoid whatever Titus had thrown and as he did so a Legionnaire grabbed his clothing and pulled him out of the saddle. The horse ran by Titus, thoroughly terrified.

"Kill or capture the horses!" a Legionnaire shouted.

Titus grabbed at the passing horse's tail. It pulled him along for a few steps then kicked back with one foot, knocking Titus backwards, threw the air. He still had some of the tail in his hands. He landed thickly on a dead horse and two dead men. One was a Legionnaire. He grabbed the man's sword.

"Thanks friend," he heard himself say.

It was done now. A few riders and handful of empty mounts had escaped.

"Grab weapons!" Carmenius ordered. "Let's move!"

Titus reached down and picked up a curved sword. He sheathed his borrowed gladius. He stepped over and on bodies and joined the mass of Legionnaires who began running again.

"Stay together!" Carmenius urged. "Stay close!"

The ran down the hill and through the grass. Titus could hear the men around him panting for breath, as he himself was.

"Halt! To ground!"

As one, the Legionnaires threw themselves to the ground. They lay there, gasping for breath, the stars twinkling down at them as the two moons watched. To Titus it seemed like the moons were enjoying this. He didn't know why he thought that, it was just how it felt. The man next to him gave him a waterskin. Titus gulped a mouthful and passed it on. Now that their breathing was quieting it seemed almost silent. Mosquitos began buzzing them. Titus ignored them.

"Crouched, go, crouched! GO!" Carmenius ordered.

Titus got to his feet again but stayed low, like the men around them. They couldn't run full out while crouched and that was a comfort. They slowed, and then stopped. In front of them was a camp. Black tents, supply wagons, a deep square pit with a few terrified skeletal humans in it. Titus recognized it- the dwarven mercenaries camp.

"They're close by," Carmenius whispered to his men.

"They have crossbows, at least two each," Titus whispered back. "They'll have slaves pulling their wagons."

The centurion smacked Titus on the arm and moved off into the mass of Legionnaires. Titus wondered what he'd done wrong before realizing that the Centurion was thanking him. Or praising him. It didn't matter anyway.

Some of the Legionnaires were motioning and whispering to the huddled figures in the pit. Titus wanted to say *don't bother*. They were likely as close to death as you could be without actually being dead.

The group of Legionnaires split into two as the 2nd century, carrying their shields came through.

"Behind the shields, lads," a different Centurion growled. "Up the hill."

Chapter 38

Every man pushed at the back of the man in front of him, creating a rising tide of shields and iron on the hillside. Titus could hear the dwarves shouting in their guttural language, along with the crack of whips. The Legionnaires were running now, and suddenly they made the hill top. The dwarven mercenaries had herded their slaves into a line in front of their wagon scorpions, which they'd turned to meet the Roman attacks. Titus threw himself to the ground and many around him did the same, imitating him. The dwarves fired the scorpions, taking off the heads of some of the slaves and punching holes into the groups of Romans. The Legionnaires surged forward regardless, pushing against the slaves who immediately gave up and let the Romans run over them. The dwarves were firing their crossbows now, killing Legionnaires everywhere. Titus was on his feet again, though he didn't remember doing it. He just knew they had to stop the dwarves from reloading the scorpions. Titus and a group of Legionnaires rushed the first wagon, which was perched on the crest of the hill. The wagon wheels had wedges to stop the wagon from moving but the force of the Legionnaires hitting it freed the wheels and the wagon rolled down the hill. Titus turn to the next one. The black bearded dwarf on it was in the control seat cranking the ratchets back. Titus stabbed forcefully into the creature's arm. The dwarf's head jerked up, his eyes wide and mouth open showing yellowed teeth. Titus stabbed again this time into the beard but it seemed he missed the dwarf's neck and body and his sword slid alongside the thick leather armor. Another Legionnaire was on the other side of the dwarf and stabbed into the little monster's neck from that side. The dwarf hollered again and reached for his own blade. Titus stabbed into the arm again and the other Legionnaire grabbed a handful of black beard and tried to pull the dwarf off the wagon. Instead the beard tore away, exposing the raw oozing flesh of the dwarf's jaw. The Legionnaire stabbed again and the dwarf fell. Titus climbed onto the scorpion and put a bolt in the channel. He swivelled until he had a dwarf with a sword in each hand standing on a wagon in his sites. He fired and the dwarf flew into the air as the bolt hit him.

"Help me!" Titus screamed at the Legionnaire who'd been finishing off the dwarf from that wagon. "Wind it! Wind it!"

The Legionnaire understood and they reloaded it and Titus fired again, closely missing a dwarf who was reloading a scorpion in the moonlight. That dwarf fired into a mass of Legionnaires and they all collapsed like a stack of sticks. Titus was reloading again and so was the other dwarf but the Legionnaire and Titus were finished first and Titus threw the bolt into the channel and fired. The shot missed the dwarf but hit his scorpion, causing one of the arms to break and fly back, hitting the dwarf, who tumbled off the wagon.

Titus and the Legionnaire reloaded again. There were no more targets. If any dwarves had survived, they were no longer in sight. The ground was crowded. with dead and injured Legionnaires, slaves and bloody dwarven bodies.

The Legionnaires didn't stop to rest though. Some were checking the corpses, stabbing the dwarves again to make sure they were dead.

"Reload the scorpions!" Centurion Carmenius ordered.

Beside him another knot of soldiers was building a fire, which Titus didn't understand initially. One of the Legionnaires began blowing a horn. The air then was filled with what looked like fireflies, glowing dots arcing high into the sky.

"Take cover!" someone called out.

"Arrows!" Carmenius roared.

Titus flipped off the wagon and rolled underneath. Before he'd stopped moving the arrows hit, thudding into the wagons and squelching into the bodies on the ground. There was another Legionnaire under the wagon and when Titus tried to climb out this other man grabbed him and held him. An instant later another volley of fire arrows hit. The flames from their oiled soaked shafts lit the hilltop like hundreds of candles showing a grotesque tableau of twisted limbs and broken horses.

Titus heard a sound he recognized- scorpions firing- the 47th's artillery must be aiming at the Ozani now. That's why they'd lit the fire, to show their position to the 47th; of course it had also show it to the horse archers.

No more arrows hit and Titus scrambled out and climbed back on to the wagon scorpion. Even in the bright moon light he couldn't see any targets. The Ozani were out there somewhere in the darkness, he just didn't know where. The sound of hooves behind him made him desperately work the gears to swivel the scorpion around.

"Hold your fire!" Centurion Carmenius roared at him. "That's the Ala."

Soon the entire 3rd cohort of the 47th arrived with shields and armor. They also had shovels and began to fortify the hill top, creating makeshift walls out of dirt, dead enemy bodies, and lifeless horses.

Titus climbed down from the wagon. Someone gave him a waterskin that was almost empty and he squeezed out the last swallow. He spent the rest of the night beside the scorpion, waiting for the order to fire. It never came. When the sky began to bleed orange he was lying in the wagon. He'd been bit by a hundred mosquitos but he didn't care. He was exhausted. As the sun peeked above the grassy horizon the full scene became visible. The top of the hill was a churned muddy mash of blood and corpses. The Legionnaires were still formed up in tight groups, their shields resting on the ground but ready. There were eleven functioning scorpion wagons. Titus saw the one that had been pushed down the hill. It had rolled on it's side and flipped over, smashing both scorpion and wagon. There was no sign of the dwarf driver.

It was a good hill for artillery. The land around was mostly flat and the little hill was the highest point in sight. There was nothing to see though. No horsemen. Just brown grass, golden where the rising sun shined on it.

The Ala began working on hooking up the captured wagon scorpions to their horses, so they could be moved faster. Legionnaires began to drag the dead into piles for burning. Two wagons from the 47th arrived with food and water. Another two wagons brought medics.

Titus looked at himself. His tunic was torn, muddy and bloody. He had a gash on his left forearm that he didn't remember getting. There was mud in his right ear. His left leg hurt like he'd been hit repeatedly with a thick stick. But he was alive. He was hungry and thirsty and he smiled and the Legionnaire beside him saw it and smiled back.

Chapter 39

"Now is not the time for resting!" Centurion Carmenius roared. "Now is the time for working!"

Titus was back with Section XII- both Tenax and Glaber. Everyone was digging, even the Immunes. They'd separated the cohorts and strung them out for miles in a long line to dig ditches and walls. The other three Legions to the North, East and West were doing the same. The Ozani were trapped in the middle.

"This isn't going to work," Glaber said.

Titus knew enough not to argue when Glaber was in such a mood. Besides he'd returned from the night mission with less to say. He was different, he realized. When you had fought hand to hand and killed and almost been killed yourself complaining about the weather or other things didn't seem that important.

"It's a long shot," Tenax agreed. "But what else is there to do? If we advance they'll just choose one flank and fill us with arrows. This way they'll have to fight their way out."

"I heard that there are ten auxiliary units on the way," Titus said as he threw his shovel full of dirt onto the earth wall.

Glaber spit. "Auxiliary units aren't worth much," he said.

"Don't let them here you say that," Tenax said.

"I'm hearing a lot of talking and not so much digging!" Carmenius shouted at them.

Titus was happy to keep quiet and dig. The area they were trying to close in was immense. If the Ozani wanted to get out- and of course they did, why would they stay? They'd have to fight their way out. That was not such a pleasant thought. Thousands of horsemen attacking a thinly manned Roman dirt fortification.

The sun was high in the sky and Titus was sweating. He paused to wipe his forehead because it was dripping into his eyes. Out further he could see Legionnaires digging small pits and placing caltrops- spiked metal, injurious to the feet of horses and men. The idea was to make the ground within arrow range of the wall very painful to walk on. Behind Titus the fortification was taking shape. First came a deep ditch, ten feet wide and as tall as a man. The dirt from all the digging was piled on the Roman side of the ditch, added another six feet of height. Centurion Carmenius had promised that sudes- sturdy wooden stakes- were coming to place on the wall as well.

Titus had seen the Ozani camp. He knew they had herds of sheep, goats and other animals. Their horses and livestock could eat the brown grass. The horsemen were used to life on the grasslands. They weren't going to be starved out quickly. The Roman's biggest concern was that the Changsammi, another large nomadic horse tribe, might try and come to the Ozani's rescue. Titus had heard that there were Roman ambassadors with the Changsammi, promising them gold to stay neutral and suggesting that their lives might be much improved if they didn't have to compete with the Ozani.

When the 4th cohort stopped for water and food the Libritors were ordered back behind the dirt wall, to begin setting up the scorpion wagons. Optio Lagois stopped by to encourage them and told them that a signal system was being put in to place so when there was an attack on the line other areas would find out quickly.

Titus was up on a wagon, aiming it out into the grass. The dwarven equipment had been claimed and he and Glaber were back to working a human made machine that didn't swivel. Tenax was paired with a Legionnaire, and a squad called Polypus had been assigned to Section XII to move the wagons as needed. The sudes hadn't arrived yet. They might never arrive, Titus thought, because that's the way things went in the Legion. Still, things looked good. The ditch was deep and the wall was high. The ground in front was filled with traps. They had a big pile of scorpion bolts. Let them come.

At sunset the Legionnaires were all ordered back behind the wall. Double watches were setup facing both directions. Titus' earlier optimism evaporated as he saw just how thinly the cohort was stretched.

"Look," Glaber said, pointing beyond the wall.

There were distant points of fire, clearly visible in the coming darkness. As the sun disappeared it seemed like the entire grassland was burning.

"I heard the Legionnaires talking about it," Glaber said. "Our troops are setting fires, trying to get it to spread and burn all of the grass. Their horses will get hungry fast."

There was a light breeze and soon the smoke began to drift over Section XII, which was all right because it helped to discourage the mosquitos. Titus' arms and legs and neck and face were already covered with itchy bites. A medic had given him a jar of cream to help. It was honey and some herbs and something else. It helped a little. He was trying not to scratch but he was constantly noticing that he was. He put his scarf over his mouth so he didn't cough too much from the smoke.

Tenax and Glaber set one of the tarps up as a tent. They did it carefully, allowing it to have flaps in an effort to keep most of the mosquitos out. The three members of Section XII lay inside. Titus thought they might chat but he quickly heard the other two snoring. Tenax sounded like a saw cutting through logs. Glaber's snore was quieter and that disturbed Titus. He thought maybe Glaber snored like a girl. The only problem was Titus had never heard a girl snore before so he didn't really know. Did girls snore? They must. They were human, similar to men. Except they weren't similar at all.

Titus didn't remember falling asleep. He woke to the sound of horns- not emergency horns but the normal get-out-of-bed-you-lazy-Legionnaires sound. He was happy that he'd slept well. Sometime in the night the sudes had arrived. There were stacks of stakes all along the wall. Titus was amazed, for he was sure they hadn't been quiet unloading them and yet he'd slept through it.

They had a quick breakfast. The air still smelled of smoke. Then they were shown how the sudes were to be mounted in the wall, making a further barrier to anyone trying to get over it. By lunch time the wooden stakes were in place and they were allowed to rest for the remainder of the afternoon. Titus fell asleep again in the tent. A sleepy Glaber roused him for supper, which was a barley porridge with a dried meat so tough it was impossible to guess what kind of animal it had come from. Still, it was good to sit and eat and wait.

"You look cranky Tenax," Glaber teased. "what's the matter, don't you like eating dried leather?"

Tenax didn't smile. "I was just thinking," he said.

"There's your problem," Glaber went on. "You should avoid thinking."

"What happens if the Ozani don't try to get out?" Tenax said.

"We wait."

Tenax shook his head. "No, we'll squeeze them more. Which means moving ahead and building this stupid wall and ditch all over again."

Chapter 40

Two days passed. They were not bad days. They were sleepy, resting and watching dust cloud days. After having been in some serious battles the inactivity didn't bother Titus. They were all desperate for news about what was happening but there were only wild rumours. A more unpleasant prospect was that they might being moving the wall forward a mile or two.

On the third morning the unpleasant rumour came true. After breakfast the 4th Cohort was formed up with shields and shovels. First they made a ramp so the wagons could cross the ditch. The Libritors along with some Legionnaires pulling moved the scorpion wagons forward.

The burnt grassland in front of the wall had been sewn with traps, but there were several narrow paths through. Titus found himself and Glaber with their wagon at the head of a column travelling down one of these clear corridors. There were three other groups travelling down similar safe paths. The entire expedition was overseen by the 4th Cohort's Senior Centurion, Titus Gavius Cezar. He was a bear of a man with an unruly black beard and a wild temper to match. They advanced through the traps and then formed up into a line and continued. Titus, who was more West than centre, could see the 3rd Cohort in the distance doing the same thing.

Cezar called a halt and the digging began. Perhaps they should have been nervous, because they were exposed with no cover, but most of the Legionnaires were stoic. More digging. Nothing to get excited about. They'd only been at it for about an hour when the lookouts saw the big dust cloud.

Soon everyone was looking and the Centurions and Optios were shouting for everyone to get back to work. The dust cloud grew bigger, closer. The Libritors were told to put their shovels down and prepare the scorpions. The Legionnaires, still shovelling, were directed to dig in front of the scorpion wagons that dotted the line. They tried to build up the earth wall as much as they could, to give the Libritors cover. Other Legionnaires were sent into the burnt grass to scatter caltrops and dig pits.

The Legionnaires dug until the last moment. The wall and ditches were only completed in front of the scorpions, so there were lots of places the horsemen would be able to ride through and around. Glaber and Titus ratcheted their scorpion and loaded it. Centurion Carmenius told them to fire at will.

The Ozani came closer and closer. When they got to the caltrops, they stopped as a few horses were injured. They seemed to be considering their options.

"Stand clear," Glaber said, and he fired.

For once Titus was able to watch the bolt sail over the ground and smash into the enemy. A man on a horse went down and the Ozani fled, like seagulls chased by children. Their dust cloud remained in sight, but Titus couldn't actually see the horsemen anymore. Everyone was ordered to resume digging. Wagons with sudes taken from the previous ditch and wall line began to arrive. Somehow having had two days of rest seemed to make working all day harder.

The centurions decided that the ditch digging would continue all night, in shifts. More Legionnaires were assigned to build traps and caltrops in front of the dirt wall too. The Libritors were excused because they were supposedly on standby all night long, ready to fire their scorpions. Section XII put up their tent and slept inside, away from the mosquitos. The noise of digging and grumbling Legionnaires didn't keep them awake.

By morning this new wall and ditch were almost complete. They worked all morning adding the sudes and then it was back to resting. Tenax predicted that they'd have two more days of rest and then they'd move the wall forward again. The Ozani still had a lot of space but they were probably feeling nervous. There was still smoke in the air from burning grass and the dust cloud made by the horsemen was always in sight.

On the second day two of the Legionnaires that were assigned to stay with the scorpion wagons got in a fight. One was named Lucas, from Polypus squad. Titus didn't know the other man. They'd been dicing, and had disagreed. It had come to blows. The rest of Polypus had quickly mobilized, grabbing both men, but they hadn't been quick enough. Centurion Carmenius was there before they could pretend nothing had happened.

Titus had always though Carmenius to be a decent Centurion. Some were bullies and some were just strange but Carmenius had always seemed reasonable. Except today.

Carmenius was shouting so much at the two men that his face went red. A group of Legionnaires had gathered to watch. They were completely silent, worry on their faces. Both of the squabblers claimed that the other was at fault. Carmenius sentenced each to five lashes. The men were stripped naked and tied to the sudes on the wall, side by side. Carmenius himself did the whipping. He started with a buttocks shot on each, then laid into their backs. He obviously knew what he was doing with a whip, for he didn't break the skin much. Neither man would have remained standing due to the pain. When Carmenius had completed five each he warned them that next time it would be ten. The men's squads came and took them down and carried them away. It was good for an afternoon's grim entertainment.

Titus, Glaber and Tenax were in the tent that night. As usual Tenax and Glaber were snoring and Titus was left wondering about how women sleep. Glaber was strong and foul-mouthed and determined and that made Titus think he was definitely male. Titus' ridiculous brother Appius had suggested that Glaber had women's legs. Titus had been looking at the Legionnaires comparatively. They'd done a lot of marching so their legs were trim and muscular, not that different than Glaber's. Just because Appius had a girlfriend didn't mean he actually knew anything about women, Titus decided.

The alarm was sounded in the middle of the night. Section XII stumbled out of their tent and rushed to their scorpions. The moons were bright and with the stars helping it was easy to watch the small group of thirty or forty horsemen struggling through the field of traps. Horses were screaming and falling, their riders crawling away and then standing and impaling their own feet on the caltrops. Even though they were the enemy it was an unpleasant sight. Carmenius had ordered the scorpions to hold their fire. No sense in wasting bolts. About twenty riders made it to the wall and surrendered. Carmenius accepted. Slaves and horses were always welcome, and the Legionnaires would all get a cut when they were sold.

The next morning they were told to move the wall forward again.

Chapter 41

This time it was clear they expected trouble. The Legionnaires advanced through the clear pathways of the trapped field with shields and pila. The scorpion wagons were near the front. The dust cloud that hung over the tribesmen was never far away now.

They could easily rush the advancing Legion.

"Get those scorpions set up!" Centurion Cezar barked.

The Libritors hurried to get their equipment ready. The Legionnaires had begun digging, but some had stayed on watch too. The diggers were working quickly, as if they expected trouble. As before they started with ditch and wall around each scorpion.

"I see them!" Glaber shouted. "They're coming."

"Shields!" the call went up from the watch.

The horse archers were advancing quickly. Glaber fired just as they released a volley of black shafts into the air. Glaber rolled out of the seat and under the wagon with Titus. The diggers dropped their tools and rushed for their shields. The arrows landed like heavy rain.

"Another volley!" someone called out.

The Libritors stayed under their scorpion wagon. They could hear the sound of the horses' hooves now.

"They're charging us!" Glaber said.

The arrows hit all around them, splintering the wood of the wagon and dinging off the metal pieces of the scorpion. They both rolled out and ratcheted. In front of them the Ozani horsemen, lances down, were just about to hit the massed Legionnaires. Titus made himself focus on reloading. He grabbed a wooden bolt and put it in the chamber. Crashes and screams erupted from in front of them. Then the sound of metal hitting metal and centurions shouting. Glaber fired and they ratcheted the scorpion back. Titus threw a bolt in the channel and Glaber fired. They ratcheted again. Titus was reaching for the bolt when Glaber shouted at him.

Titus looked up; their fortification was teardrop shaped. Many of the Ozani had smashed into the Legionnaires in front but plenty had flowed around too. There were Legionnaires on the side as well, but not as many. The Legionnaires threw their pilums, taking down the first rank of rushing horsemen. But the Ozani were not stopping and the first horsemen made contact with the Romans, lances and swords striking, stabbing. Still more horsemen pushed from behind. Titus could see their faces contorted with rage. Those that couldn't move because there was nowhere to go pulled out their bows and quickly began firing at the Legionnaires.

Titus grabbed his shield. He tried to give Glaber a shield but the young man was sitting stiffly upright in the firing seat, an arrow in his shoulder. After a moment he tumbled out onto the ground. Titus turned in time to stop a pair of arrows with his shield. Their metal heads poked through the wood. The scorpion wagon was completely surrounded now as the horsemen pushed from every side. The other Roman artillery pieces from further along the line where firing into the rear of the Ozani. Titus drew his sword and ran screaming at the nearest horse. Before he could get there a Legionnaire slashed open both the rider's leg and the horses side. The horse began bucking and flipped the rider off. The horse staggered for a moment and then collapsed.

Titus caught another arrow with his shield. He ran at the next horseman. The tribesman was fighting a Legionnaire, who suddenly fell, an arrow in his throat. The Ozani hacked down as Titus lifted his shield to block, while thrusting his gladius into the horse's unprotected side. The animal screeched and bolted.

Then it was done. The horsemen had passed them, and were riding towards the field of traps before the next wall. Titus understood their ferocious attack then. They were trying to escape.

Many Legionnaires were dead and wounded as well as many Ozani. A blood covered Legionnaire began shouting at Titus.

"Get that scorpion turned around!" he shrieked. It was the Centurion Cezar.

Titus ran back to the wagon. Glaber was moaning on the ground, still alive. A group of bloodied Legionnaires arrived and turned the wagon around. Titus made them work the ratchet as he marked, loaded and fired into the retreating Ozani. He managed two decent shots and third fell short because they were out of range.

Cezar told them to stand down. The other cohorts from either side would handle this. Besides, they had no way of knowing if there was a second wave on the way.

Legionnaires and medics began to fan out among the wounded. The soldiers were angry and killed any Ozani that they found alive. Titus knelt down by Glaber. It was an arrow in the shoulder- painful, but as long as it didn't get infected, not fatal. Glaber had been spitted- the arrow head was on one side of his shoulder and the fletching on the other, with the shaft extended right through.

Glaber looked terrified. His face was flushed red and there were tears streaming down his face. He grabbed at Titus' tunic.

"Titus- you have to help me!"

"I'll get a medic. They'll be better at it than me," he said, standing.

Glaber grabbed onto his leg. "Titus, listen to me. You need to take care of this for me."

Titus knelt down by his friend. "Glaber, you're panicking. You're going to be alright. You'll do better if you can calm down."

With his uninjured arm Glaber grabbed Titus by the hair and pulled his face close. "You don't understand," he hissed quietly. "They can't see."

"I do understand," Titus said. "Your secret is safe with me. I'll do the best that I can. You stay put and I'll go and get some advice from one of the medics."

Glaber let go of Titus' hair. "How long have you known?" she asked.

"You've got girl legs," he answered and ran to a medicus.

The combat medics were overwhelmed and had no complaint that Titus was helping out. Pull the arrow out, douse with vinegar, sew if necessary and bandage with a clean wrap. They wouldn't give Titus the vinegar but they gave him two bandage strips, and soaked one with vinegar.

Glaber was lying beside the scorpion wagon, shivering and crying.

"This is going to hurt a lot," Titus warned.

Titus studied the arrow. It looked like pulling it out would do more damage. He's scene arrow wounds like this, and watched the medicus break the arrow and pull it gently out. The arrow shaft was covered with Glaber's blood. Titus grabbed onto both ends and tried to steady the shaft before he broke it. Of course he couldn't keep it steady and Glaber screamed. While she was screaming Titus snapped the arrow and pulled the piece with the head out on one side and the piece of shaft with the fletching on the other. The wound began gushing blood. He gave the section with the arrow head to Glaber.

"Bite on it," he said. "This next part is going to hurt even more, and you scream like a girl."

Titus forced the shaft into Glaber's mouth and his friend bit down. Titus wiped the wound with the vinegar soaked rag. Glaber's body stiffened and then relaxed, as she passed out from the pain.

Chapter 42

Titus left Glaber in the care of Tenax, as all able-bodied soldiers were being ordered to advance to the rear. Tenax, aside from his limp, had been slashed down his back with a sword. It wasn't deep but it was painful and he was just sitting trying not to move. Titus put them both in the tent, left them water and reported for duty. A fifth of the available soldiers were assigned to stay put, as no one knew how many Ozani were left out in the grasslands, waiting to attack. When Titus left they were digging, rebuilding and expanding the ditch and wall and piling bodies and horses where they had to.

A group of Legionnaires were assigned to pull the scorpion wagon with all speed back towards the previous wall. Titus pushed from behind and was amazed at the speed and determination of the Legionnaires. They were angry and wanted another strike on the Ozani who'd ridden past.

They quickly came to the field that had been laid with caltrops and pits. It was now littered with dead and dying horses and a lesser number of riders' bodies. The Legionnaires stuck to the narrow clear paths and advanced quickly. Titus was breathing hard, almost running, pushing the wagon, sucking in the smell of blood and shit and death.

The dirt wall had been made to withstand riders, with it's deep ditch and wooden sudes on the wall top. The Legionnaires slowed to take in the scale of the devastation. Although the wall had only been lightly defended the Ozani had paid a terrible cost. There must have been a thousand dead horses. The buzz of flies was so loud they could barely hear the Centurions shouting at them to keep going.

They avoided the breech in the wall. There was actually a pool of blood at the bottom of the pile of twisted men and slaughtered horses. It was too much for the ground to soak up. It looked like the Ozani had just tried to ride over the wall. One dead horse was still standing on top of the wall, somehow impaled on several of the wooden stakes.

"Keep moving!" Centurion Carmenius shouted.

Titus and the Legionnaires made a second breech, and dragged the wagon up. There was another column 200 feet away doing the same thing. The Legionnaires made quick work of constructing a ramp, as they'd brought a number of shovels with them.

They continued moving once they'd passed the wall. There was a trail of Ozani bodies- those that had been wounded and could go no further- that led to the next field of traps. Although some of the caltrops had been removed and used again on the previous wall there were still pits and some caltrops. Accordingly there were dead horses and riders.

"Scorpions!" Carmenius shouted.

On the other side of the field of traps several thousand horsemen were battering against the wall. They weren't through yet. They quickly set up the scorpions. A Legionnaires named Tullus had been assigned to ratchet with Titus. He didn't say much and had a purple bruise on the side of his face. His arms worked fine though and they loaded the scorpion and waited for orders.

Another Legionnaire ran up- a messenger. "Centurion says there's Auxiliary Troops on this wall, so aim lower. Fire at will." He ran off to inform the next scorpion crew.

Titus aimed as instructed and fired. It was impossible to see the impact in the writhing mass of Ozani struggling at the wall. They reloaded and fired again. And four more times. There was a visible reaction now. The Ozani were abandoning the wall and riding through the field of traps. Numerous horses stepped in the holes and stumbled, some breaking their legs and throwing their riders.

"Shield wall!" Carmenius shouted.

The Legionnaires rushed to line up in front of the scorpions, shields out. Titus had to jump off the wagon and run after Tullus. He caught the man's arm and gave him a pull back towards the scorpion.

"We need to keep firing! I can't load it without you!"

They ran back and ratcheted the weapon. You could hear the

hooves now, and the ground was shaking.

"Arrows!" Someone yelled.

Titus fired the bolt in the channel and looked up to see how much time he had before he had to roll under the wagon. The arrows went high and then dropped down on to the charging Ozani. They were Roman arrows! There must be auxiliary troops on the other side of the wall. Titus and Tullus ratcheted the rope back, loaded and fired again.

The Ozani horsemen rode into the Legionnaires. None of them had lances -they were attacking with swords and arrows. Titus fired again, saw the bolt lift a man out of the saddle and throw him away. The Roman arrows kept falling, but they were aiming for the middle of the trapped field, so they didn't hit the Legionnaires.

The enemy horsemen seemed to run out of steam; those in the front were cut down and the reminder turned and charged back at the wall again.

"4th Cohort advance!" Carmenius shouted. "Ware of caltrops and pits!"

The Legionnaires slowly walked forward, around the fresh dead. Titus fired off another shot and they reloaded.

"Should we advance?" Tullus asked. It was the first time Titus had heard him speak. His voice was thick, probably because his face was swollen.

"We've no pullers and they're in range," Titus said. "So no." Titus fired and they reloaded.

The dwindling number of horsemen ran around, looking for an escape. Some came at the Legionnaires. Some attempted the wall. There was a sizeable number of Ozani on foot now, and they'd formed into a large group and were trying to dig at the wall. The archers were targeting them and they were falling like Autumn leaves in a stiff wind. Titus and Tullus moved the wagon so that Titus could fire bolts into the horseless Ozani as well. They were an easier target, as they didn't move as fast as horsemen.

Like every battle that Titus had been in, the end was sudden. There were very few Ozani left. Some of the were crazed, running at the wall and being killed, others seemed exhausted- wounded, winded, slow moving. They refused to surrender. Titus felt the battle rage leave his body. When you were fighting for your life or your comrades', killing was the only thing in your head. Now Titus felt bad for the last few Ozani. They should surrender. They didn't. The Auxiliary archer unit on the other wall shot the last of them. Titus raised his fist in the air and cheered with the rest of the Romans.

Chapter 43

They marched back to the newest wall under construction in force. The Legionnaires of the 47th were joined by the 1st Kukumerlant auxiliaries; archers who wore chain mail and white hoods- which had given them their nickname. Accompanying the White Hoods was the 4th Brynn, a light infantry auxiliary cohort.

Titus was relieved to find both Tenax and Glaber still alive. Tenax looked much improved and Glaber much worse. The older black bearded man had good color and was hungry. Glaber looked pale and only answered question with moany one word answers. Titus touched her face- funny that touching Glaber's face was different now that she was female- anyway she was feverish. He promised to fetch a medicus but she argued it.

"They'll want to look at the wound," she moaned. "They'll find out."

Titus didn't say anything, just nodded. He wasn't going to argue. Female or not, Glaber was his best friend. When he left the tent he found a medicus and reported that Glaber had a fever and was delirious. The medic went to fetch some silphium. Titus joined a group that was marching out further into the interior of the grasslands. He felt sad that he preferred facing the enemy over helping Glaber He'd gone against her wishes though, and he didn't want to face her anger. If she lived. As he pushed the wagon scorpion and the Legionnaires pulled, Titus wondered if their friendship would survive. Maybe no one else would discover her gender. She'd gotten this far, it was possible she could continue. Sadly he didn't think he could ever by quite the same around her again.

Centurion Cezar which in charge of the advance party, which contained the wagon scorpions. The orders were simple- find the

Ozani camp and subdue it. Slaves were desired, as were any horses. The Ozani mounts were small when compared to the typical Roman horse, but they were sturdy, resilient and worth many times more than no horses at all.

In the distance they saw a dust cloud. Scouts informed that it was forces of the 22nd Legion *Magnum*, advancing just the same as they were. The 47th picked up the pace. When they finally sited the Ozani tents there was no dust or campfire smoke hovering over it.

Cezar called for a line. The Legionnaires dashed into position. The 47th wanted to be the first to the Ozani camp- first come, first loot, first slaves. The wagon scorpions were deployed in the very front, even ahead of the Legionnaires. Centurion Cezar wanted to scare the Ozani. Titus would have preferred to have been behind the shield wall, but orders were orders.

The 47th stood for a moment, waiting for some kind of response from the Ozani. The camp looked the same as Titus had recalled- tents here and there placed with no plan or intention. It seemed very quiet- not surprising, since most of the occupants would be elderly, female or young. They were probably hiding in their tents. When there was no response Centurion Cezar ordered an advance.

Titus climbed down from the firing seat and pushed at the rear of the wagon as the Legionnaires pulled it forward. He'd been paired with Tullus again, who still seemed quiet and nervous. When they'd covered a quarter of the distance they halted and Titus mounted the scorpion again.

The camp was unnaturally quiet. Silent even. Something was wrong. Had it been abandoned or was it a trap of some kind?

They advanced again, cutting by half their distance from the Ozani tents. The dust cloud from the advancing 22nd Legion was getting closer. Centurion Cezar ordered them to form columns and then to advance into the Ozani camp with pila ready. Titus knew he should stay with the scorpion wagon but Tullus was going and Titus was curious. He was also interested in seeing if there was anything valuable.

Four columns of Legionnaires poured into the Ozani camp, Titus in the far West line. The Auxiliary units held their positions at the rear.

The Legionnaires stayed together and the centurions kept

shouting at them. Titus could see that individual Legionnaires wanted to break away and search through the tents while the centurions were more interested in staking out the whole area for the 4th Cohort. The columns were halted and specific instructions given about what could be kept and what had to be handed in to the centurions. That loot would be divided up and paid out with their wages. Titus could see the tents swaying slightly with the breeze. They hung limply, unnaturally. A slightly stronger gust showed that they'd all been slit. Cut top to bottom in many places to render them useless as tents. It was a harbinger of what was to come.

When the Legionnaires were finally given release to search and loot they found the tents all had bodies in them. The women, children, slaves and elderly lay in neat rows, their throats slit. There was no sign of any valuables. Liquids were poured out, foods mixed with dirt. The Ozani had known they were going to lose, and had done their best to poison any victory the Romans might have.

Titus saw a slashed tent with eight children and three women inside. They'd been dead long enough for the blood to have pooled and thickened. The flies were already there but there was so much food for them there were no great concentrations. Someone said that all the herd animals had been slaughtered and their bodies covered with their excrement. Titus found the scope of it sickening. The men had ridden into the walls and traps, determined to escape or die. They'd left nothing behind. The Ozani as a tribe were annihilated.

They'd all seen dead people before; most times the Legionnaires had been the ones that had done the killing. This was different. Some of the soldiers were angry, and they kicked at the tents and dead bodies. Others appeared lost and confused. Titus was in the latter group. He thought not of the lost booty but of his brothers. Imagined escorting them to a tent, watching them, the three of them together slicing up the tent. And then making them comfortable and killing them. He felt dizzy and had to sit down.

Centurion Cezar was angry. He was cursing and swearing and shaking his fists at the cloudless sky. He walked out of the camp of the dead and went back to the auxiliary units, where he had a cornicen sound the recall. Slowly, like children being called back from a day at the beach, the Legionnaires drifted away and formed up in front of the auxiliaries.

"Should we send a messenger to the 22nd to tell them?" an Optio asked.

Cezar swore again. "Landica! Flocci non facio! Let the caudex rancens find out for themselves!"

They marched back to the nearest partially finished wall, the Legionnaires walking slower and not in step. It was done. They were finally letting go of all the tension that had been keeping them standing. Cezar dismissed them all as the Auxiliary units set out to man the outer wall.

Chapter 44

Tenax looked even better when Titus arrived at the tent. He was standing and walking- very slowly, but it was improvement. Glaber wasn't in the tent.

"She's gone," Tenax said. "Did you know she was a woman?"

Titus just shook his head. He knew and he didn't know. It hadn't mattered and he hated that now it did.

"Where'd she go?"

"The medicus examined her. Then he brought Janus," Tenax explained. "She went with the Centurion."

Titus began to ask around. Janus was Centurion of the 6th Century of the 4th Cohort. He was a massive man with a bald head, a short beard and an angry demeanor. He'd been left in charge when the rest of the cohort had marched out because no one really liked Janus, or at least that was Titus' theory.

The camp had an entirely different spirit to it now that the fighting was over. Things were still neatly laid out but the Legionnaires seemed dull and drowsy. There were no dice games and no arguing. Titus was directed to Janus' tent where the 6th Century was camped. The Centurion himself was standing outside his tent, arms crossed, wild eyes watching everything around him. Titus walked up and saluted.

"Sir!" Titus sir. "I'm a Libritor from section XII. Inquiry about my comrade Glaber, sir."

Titus was tall but Janus was half a head taller. He was also built like a small mountain. He looked down at Titus, his expression unchanging.

"There's no such person," he said flatly.

A series of nightmarish possibilities fluttered through Titus' mind- all of them ending with Glaber raped and dead. He focused his eyes on the Centurion again. On the Centurion's eyes.

"Sir! I'm looking for person who was pretending to be Glaber, sir."

The Centurion squinted at him. "Why?"

"Glaber was my best friend, sir. We were a scorpion team. I just want to know if Glaber is all right, sir."

Centurion Janus seemed to think about it. "Wait," he said.

Janus turned and went to his tent. He opened the flap quickly and stepped in. Titus was sure that he saw another person in the tent. He wondered if the big Centurion was holding Glaber against her will. Titus wondered what he could do about it. Janus was obviously stronger and a better fighter. If Titus wanted to get past him the best bet was to kill Janus quickly. He drew his gladius and held it by his side. The throat was the best target. He took a quick look around. The 6th Century were idling around the surrounding tents. Titus wondered if they'd come to their Centurion's defence, or would they cheer his downfall?

Janus stepped out of the tent. He still had the same expression as when Titus had arrived. Titus wasn't sure what it was- simmering anger perhaps? Like a coiled snake, capable of striking out quickly at any moment.

"Go into the tent," Janus said. "It's my tent, treat it with respect."

Titus nodded. "Yes sir! Thank you sir!"

Janus smiled at him. The man had a rather disturbing grin. "Put your sword away unless you're going to use it."

"Yes sir!"

Titus resheathed his gladius. He stepped over to the tent, opened the flap and went inside. Glaber was sitting there. She wasn't wearing her chain mail, or her tunic. There was a thick bandage around her shoulder, and beneath that a tight band of fabric covering the place where her breasts would be. Titus was suddenly at a loss for words. He sat down opposite her, but five feet away.

"I'm sorry," Titus said. "I'm really sorry."

Glaber just looked at him. He couldn't tell what her expression meant.

"It was me who sent the medicus," Titus said. "This is all my fault."

Glaber smiled a little. "The wound was infected," she said. "Who ever cleaned it out the first time didn't do a very good job."

Of course it was Titus who'd done it. "My fault again," he said softly.

"It's okay, Titus," she said. "It was good while it lasted. I guess I couldn't fool everyone forever."

Relieved, Titus smiled. Glaber smiled back at him.

"Is Janus..." Titus didn't know how to say it. "How is he treating you?"

"Like a big brother," she said. "I'll be fine until we get back to Dertona."

"Then what?"

Her smiled faded. "Then I'm out. Expelled from the Legion."

"You can go to my farm," Titus said all at once. "My families' farm. My brothers are decent and they could use an adult's help."

"I think Appius is already taking care of everything," she said.

"I just meant- I know that you probably need a place to go- you could go there- just for a while- if you needed to, I mean."

Glaber reached out her hand and Titus scooted closer and took it. He was going to say that she was the best friend he'd ever had but then he noticed that she was already quietly crying and so he decided to keep his mouth shut.

"I'm sorry for everything," Titus said.

It made Glaber cry even more.

Janus must have had rabbit ears for he grumbled outside the tent "Do I need to come in there?"

"No sir," Glaber said. She let go of Titus' hand. "I'll think about it," she said.

Titus nodded, smiling.

Chapter 45

The 47th stayed on the grasslands for another two days, though Titus wasn't sure why. They packed their gear up, ready to march out, burned the Roman dead and rested. They left the big Ozani camp alone. Titus could smell the rot every time the wind blew the right way and there was a constant cloud of black birds hovering and landing. Rations increased, and wine was given out, courtesy of Senior Tribune Politio, who was very proud of them. They'd fought bravely and like true Romans, the Centurions told them. There would be a bonus pay out once they arrived at their base in Dertona.

Titus didn't visit Glaber again. He walked by once but Janus gave him such an evil eye Titus kept going. He knew she was safe. That was worth a lot.

Some of the auxiliary units were busy constructing a base. They were going to stay for a while, apparently. Poor suckers. Hope they enjoyed grass.

When the horns woke them on the third day everyone was ready to go. They didn't rush but they didn't dawdle either. Titus and Tenax had a squad of Legionnaires to move the two scorpion wagons. Tenax still wasn't recovered and limped along behind his while Titus pushed at the other one. The pace was moderate, almost enjoyable. Titus looked around a lot, though there was only brown grass and blue sky to watch. The trip had a site-seeing air about it.

In the afternoon on the second day they saw a group of horsemen on a near hill watching them. It was startling- they hadn't been called to be prepared or anything. Word passed through the column that it was the Changsammi- the tribe that hadn't joined with the Ozani. They seemed quite happy to see the Romans leaving.

The closer they got to Dertona the more excited Titus became. He'd get to go on leave and see his brothers and Glaber, who he hadn't seen at all since that time in the tent. He was hopeful. Maybe he didn't have to lose his best friend after all.

As usual the streets of Dertona were lined with families, friends and prostitutes, looking for their loved ones in the Legion. The gates of the base were open and Titus was happy to pass between them. They were marched to the big parade ground at the center of the base. The centuries that had stayed behind were waiting there, all clean and shiny and standing at attention. Titus was hoping that they'd be dismissed immediately but it didn't happen. The platform that officers used to give speeches was in position- apparently the Legion was going to have to suffer that before they were dismissed.

Titus was standing near the back, besides Tenax. The Libritors always got stuck at the rear. Titus didn't mind so much. You had to stand still and look pretty in the front. The further back you were the less discipline there was.

Titus had learned to recognize the Senior Tribune, having seen him several times during the campaign. It wasn't Politio who stepped up onto the dais.

"Welcome back 47th Legion!" the man shouted. "I am your new commanding officer, Legate Decimius Aurelius Sebastian." He was average height, black hair and beard- which was surprising. Most of the officers were clean shaven in the style of the Emperor these days. The Legate was barrel chested but he also looked like he hadn't been very active recently.

It wasn't really a surprise. Everyone knew that the Senior Tribune was a relative of the Emperor, and as such he wouldn't be trusted with a Legion for long, in case he got purple ideas.

"I have good news for you and bad news," the new Legate boomed.

There was grumbling in the ranks and the Centurions let it pass. The Legate on the platform waited until it was quiet before speaking again.

"The bad news is that the 47th is being moved."

An actual chorus of boos and groans broke out, which the Centurions quelled with their vine canes.

"In two weeks' time we will began deployment to the province of Eastern Calbania," the Legate announced.

Tenax groaned.

"Where's that?" Titus asked quietly.

"The Eastern edge of the Empire," Tenax said. "A fucking desert."

"The good news is that you're all to receive a bonus and one weeks leave before we go," the Legate said.

There were cheers now. There was going to be money in

everyone's pocket and a week to blow it all. They were dismissed after that. The Libritors went to the artillery headquarters to see to the wagon scorpions and to complain. Half of the artillery men were happy to go. Some of the unhappy ones had families in the area, like Titus. There was also that group that was never happy and complained about everything.

"This is punishment," Mergo from Section VIII was whining.

"Why would we be punished?" someone asked.

"Not us, Politio. He's got a Legion behind him now so the Emperor is going to stick us as far away as possible." Mergo spat on the ground.

Titus didn't say anything. He and Tenax gathered the left over bolts and bundled them up and put them inside the storehouse. They made sure the leather covers were on the scorpions and that water couldn't get in to ruin the ropes. Then they went to their barracks.

Glaber's few belongings were all gone. They would have kicked her out quietly and as quick as possible. Titus hoped that they'd paid her what she was entitled to receive.

Titus and Tenax divided the few things that had been Capio's.

"You all right?" Tenax asked, surprising Titus.

"Yea. I just thought we'd be staying here for a while," Titus answered. "I have family here."

Tenax nodded and lay down on his bed. After a few moments, Titus did the same.

Chapter 46

As usual Titus had to wait until nearly the end for his leave. He had the bonus money in his pocket when he went out the gate and practically ran to his family's farm. There was no one in the house when he got there, which wasn't surprising. They'd be out working. He took a quick look around. There were only two beds.

He didn't want to go and look for his brothers. He stayed at the house, sitting by the front door, looking at the sky. It was filled with big white fluffy clouds, completely unlike the sky above the brown grassland. Maybe he was looking for something in the sky;

hope, purpose, reason. None of that was there. Just fluffy white clouds.

Titus' youngest brother Tullus was the first one to come back. He dropped the firewood he was carrying when he saw Titus and rushed at him, grabbing him in a hug that made Titus smile. Tullus spilled all the news- things were going fine, Appius had gotten engaged to Letitia, the girl across the river. They were planning a wedding. Appius walked up then. He looked even taller, though he was of course not as tall as Titus. The two shook hands like men and Titus presented Appius with the bonus money.

"That's for your wedding," Titus said.

Appius smiled and hugged him.

They went inside and Tullus began to prepare supper.

"Anyone stop by, any messages?" Titus asked.

Both his brother's shook their heads. Titus had already known, but he had to ask. Just in case.

The end

About the author

Itten Sylvano is interested in action adventure and historical military combined with fantasy and alternate history elements.

Sylvano's other books

HOLD THE LINE
Fifty years ago the two countries of Casteran and Nidol fought a bitter war. Casteran prevailed and over the decades the uneasy peace has grown into a tolerant trading partnership.
Newly commissioned Casteranian Captain Andrew Cutter, son of the hated and famous retired General Cutter, receives his first posting to Madlow, a hopeless dead end remnant of the last war.
Newly commissioned Nidolise Daluav Victoria Sels, daughter of First Minister Aloysius Sels, receives her first posting to the until now quiet disputed border area of Madlow.
Madlow changes everything.

BLOODY BLUE SKIES
A dark secret stalks young dwarf Taneyth Grouvenson. He and his mother reside in the small remote outpost of Merrtop, which guards a gate to the massive underground dwarven tunnel system. His father disappeared before he was born and the little family has stayed in the last place they saw him, never giving up hope for his return.
But blind hope is not enough to hold Tanyeth there and one night the beardling runs away with a group of passing dwarven mercenaries, The Sky Blues. As they travel he experiences

firsthand the machinations of war, the fickleness of other races and the awakening of his own dark secret.

THE RED HANDKERCHIEF

A young woman is found stabbed to death in her apartment, a red handkerchief stuffed in her mouth. When a second woman is found murdered in the same way the police begin hunting for a serial killer.

Detectives Steven Hodgeson and John Moore are assigned to the task force investigating the case. But Moore can't shake the gut feeling that something's wrong. Hodgeson isn't sure if his partner is right, or if Moore himself is becoming dangerously unhinged.

I. Sylvano

Made in the USA
Middletown, DE
27 October 2022

13623799R00085